"You'll see how lived-in things get with kids around," Elisabeth said.

That should have slammed the brakes on what Henry was feeling for Elisabeth. Beautiful, gorgeous, sexy. She was all those things and more, and he didn't understand why the rest of the package—waitress with a farm and three siblings—wasn't putting a damper on his attraction to her.

Sure they weren't her kids, but with her parents gone, they might as well be. And he avoided women with children. He didn't want innocent bystanders getting hurt once the relationship came to an end. And it always came to an end. He couldn't help himself. And besides, soon he would have to return to his *real* life in the *real* world.

A good reason to keep his distance from his appealing boss. No matter his attraction, it couldn't go further. There would be *no* flirting.

So why did his resolution send regret inching its way down his spine?

Dear Reader,

In this month of tricks or treats, there's no magic to delivering must-read love stories each month. We simply publish upbeat stories from the heart and hope you find them a treat.

What can you do to keep these great stories coming? Plenty! You can write me or visit our online community at www.eHarlequin.com and let me know the stories you like best. Or if you have trouble finding the latest Silhouette Romance titles, be sure to remind your local bookseller how much you enjoy them. This way you will never miss your favorites.

For example, IN A FAIRY TALE WORLD… combines classic love stories, a matchmaking princess and a sprinkling of fairy-tale magic for all-out fun! Myrna Mackenzie launches this Silhouette Romance six-book series with *Their Little Cowgirl* (#1738)—the story of a cowboy and urban Cinderella who lock horns and then hearts over his darling baby daughter.

In *Georgia Gets Her Groom!* (#1739), the latest in Carolyn Zane's THE BRUBAKER BRIDES series, Georgia discovers that Mr. Wrong might be the right man for her, after all. Then watch what happens when a waitress learns her new ranch hand is a tycoon in disguise, in *The Billionaire's Wedding Masquerade* (#1740) by Melissa McClone. And if you like feisty heroines and the wealthy heroes that sweep them off their feet, you'll want to read *Cinderella's Lucky Ticket* by Melissa James (#1741).

Read these romance treats and share the love and laughter with Silhouette Romance this month!

Mavis C. Allen
Associate Senior Editor, Silhouette Romance

Please address questions and book requests to:
Silhouette Reader Service
U.S.: 3010 Walden Ave., P.O. Box 1325, Buffalo, NY 14269
Canadian: P.O. Box 609, Fort Erie, Ont. L2A 5X3

The Billionaire's Wedding Masquerade

MELISSA McCLONE

SILHOUETTE *Romance*®

Published by Silhouette Books

America's Publisher of Contemporary Romance

To Amy, Betsy, Shirley and Virginia

Thanks to Brent and Vanessa at LaFollettes Berry Farm,
Jenny Andersen, Dr. Terry Sedgewick and Dave Working
for answering my questions.
Any mistakes are mine.

SILHOUETTE BOOKS

ISBN 0-373-19740-3

THE BILLIONAIRE'S WEDDING MASQUERADE

Books by Melissa McClone

Silhouette Romance

If the Ring Fits... #1431
The Wedding Lullaby #1485
His Band of Gold #1537
In Deep Waters #1608
The Wedding Adventure #1661
Santa Brought a Son #1698
The Billionaire's Wedding Masquerade #1740

Yours Truly

Fiancé for the Night

MELISSA McCLONE

With a degree in mechanical engineering from Stanford University, the last thing Melissa McClone ever thought she would be doing is writing romance novels, but analyzing engines for a major U.S. airline just couldn't compete with her "happily-ever-afters."

When she isn't writing, caring for her three young children or doing laundry, Melissa loves to curl up on the couch with a cup of tea, her cats and a good book. She enjoys watching home-decorating shows to get ideas for her house—a 1939 cottage that is *slowly* being renovated.

Melissa lives in Lake Oswego, Oregon, with her own real-life hero husband, two daughters, son, two lovable but oh-so-spoiled indoor cats and a no-longer-stray outdoor kitty who decided to call the garage home. Melissa loves to hear from readers. You can write to her at P.O. Box 63, Lake Oswego, OR 97034.

HENRY'S TO DO LIST

1. Turn off the water

2. Milk the cow

3. Fall in love

4. Move the irrigation equipment

5. Mow between the berry rows

6. Propose

7. Unload the hay bales

8. Gather the eggs

9. Feed the animals

10. Make all the Wheeler family's dreams come true

Chapter One

"What are you smiling about, Henry?" Cade Waters, attorney turned child advocate, sat across from him in the red-vinyl booth. "Hole-in-the-wall cafés are more my style than yours."

Henry Davenport stared at the nubile blond waitress. "Not with her working here."

"Not your usual type," Cade said.

True, but Henry wanted her. Take away the pink knee-length skirt, the white shirt, the stained apron, the ugly white shoes and the nude-colored support hose not even his housekeeper would be caught dead in, and she'd be perfect. Almost naked, too, which would make her all the more perfect.

He grinned at the thought. Perhaps it was too much to imagine she wore a lacy underwire bra and matching thong, but hey, this was his daydream and the waitress had to spend her tips on something. What better than sexy lingerie?

"Thank you, Cynthia, for suggesting we stop here," Henry said. "I'm certain the food will be delicious. The view is *très magnifique*."

"I only wanted to eat before we went wine tasting." Cade's bride-to-be, Cynthia Sterling, pursed her glossed lips. "Would you actually consider asking a waitress out?"

"Why not?" Henry asked. "I've dated actresses, models, dancers and socialites. Even you, darling."

"Only once. Thank goodness."

Cade placed a protective arm around his fiancée. "Lucky for me the two of you were more like brother and sister than boyfriend and girlfriend."

She leaned against him. "Lucky for me I met you."

The tenderness of Cynthia's smile touched Henry's heart. Once again his matchmaking skills had been perfect. No fine-tuning or adjustment needed. There were few things Henry truly enjoyed, but seeing his friends find true love topped the list. And no one could argue with his success.

"What do you think your relationship would be with the waitress, Henry?" Cynthia asked.

"Maybe he wants to hire her." Cade raised a brow. "Have her wear one of those little black French maid outfits and give her a feather duster."

"A feather duster." Henry grinned at the image forming in his mind. "I like that."

Cynthia rolled her eyes. "I doubt it's your furniture you want dusted."

Cade laughed and patted Cynthia's hand. As her diamond engagement ring sparkled, Henry noticed her French manicure. "Your fingernails have grown back."

"Finally," Cynthia said, flexing her fingers. "After your deserted-island adventure, I never thought my hands would look the same. Though I still have a few calluses."

Cade kissed the top of her hand. "Just a reminder of what we had to go through to find each other."

Every year on April Fools' Day, Henry threw himself a birthday party and sent two of his friends on an adventure of a lifetime where he set them up to fall in love. It was the best way he knew to insure his friends' happiness. "A small price to pay for happily-ever-after."

"A small price?" Cynthia frowned. "I ended up with a bamboo pole stuck in my foot and had surgery."

"I'm sorry about your foot." Henry still sent her a bouquet of flowers each week to make up for her injury. "But that was a freak accident. No one else has ever gotten hurt."

"Accidents do happen." Cynthia narrowed her eyes. "Who knows what will happen during your next adventure?"

"Two people will fall in love." Henry rubbed his palms together. "Just like you did. And Brett and Laurel Matthews, too. Admit it, darling. I've become an accomplished matchmaker."

"Two happy couples and you've let success go to your head." Cynthia sighed. "I suppose you want us to call you Cupid."

"Cupid has a nice ring," he admitted. "But I prefer Henry."

Cynthia leaned forward. "You know, Henry, it isn't right to play around with people's lives this way."

"It is right, darling." Henry flashed her his most dazzling smile. Of course, she was immune to the effect, but perhaps the waitress caught a glimpse. He loved flirting and the nuances that went with it. "In fact, it's my duty to those I care most about. If not for me, you wouldn't be engaged."

Cade nodded. "He's got a point, Sterling."

"I'm grateful for you introducing me to Cade, but there has to be an easier way to find love than having you play puppet master with your adventures." She spoke with tenderness and Henry knew she wasn't trying to offend him. "Someone could get hurt. Not just an injured foot, but a broken heart. Or worse."

"Don't tell me you want me to stop my adventures?"

"I won't tell you," Cynthia said. "But I do."

"My friends would be too disappointed if I stopped."

"Not all your friends," Cade admitted. "You do enough for your friends by planning trips and parties and all sorts of other fun things. The adventures aren't necessary."

"They are necessary." At first Henry had planned his adventures to keep himself and his friends entertained. But once he saw how good he was at executing them and how much his friends enjoyed them and how successful he was at matchmaking and how wonderful it was to have a godchild… "I'm not stopping."

"It's time you entered the real world, Henry," Cynthia said. "If you knew what being sent on an adventure was like you would change your tune."

"I would love to be sent on an adventure."

"You would?" Cynthia asked.

"Be careful how you answer," Cade cautioned.

"Of course, it would be fun," Henry said without any hesitation. No one would ever go to the effort to create an adventure for him. It was too much work. No one had that kind of free time. Not the way he did.

Cynthia straightened. "I'm so happy to hear you say that."

The beautiful young waitress stepped from the kitchen and walked his way. The seductive sway of her hips hypnotized him. He focused on her heart-shaped face. A pair of blue eyes met his. Clear and bright, her gaze made Henry straighten.

"Welcome to the Berry Bistro." She greeted him with a wide smile and he sucked in a breath. "I'm Elisabeth, may I take your order?"

Her voice was soft, perfect for whispering sweet and not-so-sweet words into his ear. "Do you have any specials that could possibly compare to your dazzling smile, Lizzie?"

He expected her to flirt back. Women always did. Instead she pressed her lips together. "No specials this morning, and it's Elisabeth with an *S*."

Not just a pretty face. Charm alone was not going to win her over. He liked that. Most women simply fell at his feet. And wallet. "My mistake, Elisabeth with an *S*."

She readied her pencil. "Your order?"

The only thing Henry wanted was her. Nothing else mattered at this moment. Not food, water, oxygen—strike that. He never gave up oxygen. It must be the challenge he found so appealing.

"Would you like to order?" Elisabeth asked again.

"Give us a minute, please," Cade said.

"I'd love some bottled water," Cynthia said. "Do you have Pellegrino?"

Elisabeth's shoulders sagged. "I'm sorry, we don't."

"That's okay," Cynthia said with a reassuring tone. "Just bring whatever you have and lemon wedges, too."

As Elisabeth walked away, Henry felt an urge to follow her, even if it meant stepping into what no doubt was a greasy, smelly kitchen. He leaned back against the booth.

A challenge was one thing. This was…different. The strength of attraction took him by surprise. Lately it seemed to take something extravagant or someone larger than life to work up his interest. Not that anything appealed to him for long.

Cynthia stared at him. "Are you honestly attracted to that work-hard-to-make-it-look-natural, girl-next-door kind of look?"

"I'd say everything about Elisabeth with an *S* is as natural as it gets," Cade admitted before Henry had the chance.

The words earned him a good-hearted elbow from Cynthia. "I'm the only natural girl for you."

"Of course you are," Cade said. "But a man can look."

And enjoy, Henry thought.

On her way to the kitchen, Elisabeth picked up vases from the empty tables. In her crisp white shirt, with her hands full of flowers, she looked like a bride. Henry got a flash of her wearing a wedding gown made from the finest white silk, with a flowing veil held in place by an intricately woven floral wreath and a coordinating bouquet of flowers in her hands. He wasn't simply imagining her as any bride. He was imagining Elisabeth as his bride. The tenderness of the image surprised him. The reality of the thought terrified him. He didn't do brides.

He had it bad.

But bad didn't begin to describe how a waitress from a blink-and-you'll-miss-it town on the edge of Oregon's Yamhill wine country had left Henry speechless and shaking in his Churches. "Let's find another restaurant."

Two small lines formed above Cynthia's nose. "What's wrong with this one?"

"The service," he said.

"I'm the one who asked her to give us a minute," Cade said.

"It can't be the waitress," Cynthia added. "You said she was lovely."

"No, I mean, yes, she is lovely. But I didn't say it. Well, I just did, but not before." Henry shifted in his seat. "Can we just go?"

"Well, well, well. This is an interesting turn of events." A smug smile formed on Cynthia's lips. "Of all the women in the world, a waitress from some Podunk town is the one who has finally spooked the world's most confirmed bachelor."

"I'm not spooked." But as Henry said the words he knew he was more than spooked, and he wanted it to stop. Now.

"You're pale," Cade added.

Henry raised his chin. "I'm hungry."

"Then we should stay and eat so we can leave your waitress a nice big tip," Cynthia said.

"She's not my waitress. I'm not interested in her."

"I've never seen a woman have an effect on you like this." Mischief gleamed in Cynthia's eyes. "You really like her."

"I like the look of her. I don't know her. And I won't be getting to know her." Henry glanced toward the kitchen and hoped her shift was over. "Elisabeth's a waitress. I'm a… I'm me. What would we talk about?"

Cade laughed. "You want to talk to her?"

He had a point. The image of her nearly nude and brandishing a feather duster was etched on Henry's brain. But he didn't want to think about that. He didn't want to think about the things they could do together. He didn't want to think about her.

"I don't want to talk to her," Henry said. "I don't want anything to do with her. Can we go?"

"Oh, knock it off." Cynthia nudged Cade. "Excuse me, honey, I need to powder my nose."

As she slid out of the booth, Henry fiddled with his paper napkin. "Elisabeth seems…sweet. Innocent."

"That's never stopped you before," Cynthia said before walking away.

It hadn't. And made the situation clearer. The sooner Henry put Elisabeth with an *S* and this two-bit little town behind him, the better.

As Elisabeth placed a bottle of water on her tray, her hand trembled. She couldn't believe the guy from table four, who looked like a movie star with his expressive hazel-green eyes and killer smile, had been flirting with her. And she couldn't believe she'd shut him down. Stupid move, but she hadn't been thinking straight. She hadn't been thinking at all.

She should have played along, done all those flirty things she used to know how to do and gotten a big, fat tip. The trio at table four had money. The shoes were always a giveaway.

Kathy Alexander placed a small plate of lemon wedges on the tray. "Here you go."

"Thanks."

Kathy owned the Berry Bistro, which until two weeks ago and for the past nineteen years had been called Kathy's Korner Kafe. Berry Patch, Oregon, wanted to become upscale to appeal to wine country visitors. Of course, the bistro was still a corner café. For now. "Is this for table four?"

Elisabeth nodded.

"Those two men are lookers. Especially the guy with the light brown hair and brown eyes."

"Hazel," Elisabeth corrected. "His eyes are hazel."

She hadn't liked being stared at with those eyes. His gaze had been so intense, so intimate. Elisabeth had felt exposed, naked and had wanted to run away.

"He called me Lizzie." She'd been called Beth, Bess, Bessey, Lissie and Lis. Those names didn't bother her. But Lizzie… "Every time I hear that name I think of Lizzie Borden chopping up her parents with an ax. It gives me the willies."

"He could call me whatever he wanted, and I'd answer." Kathy sighed. "Sure would like a taste of that eye candy."

"He's too much of a pretty boy."

"I remember when you used to love pretty boys."

And look where that had gotten her. Elisabeth tightened her grip on the tray. "That was a long time ago."

"Not that long ago, honey." Kathy stared at her. "And that pretty boy at table four looked as if the only thing he wanted to order was you."

"I'm not on the menu."

"Maybe you should be." Kathy's eyes darkened with concern. "Have you found someone to fill in for Manny?"

"No." Manny Gallegos ran the berry farm for Elisabeth. Between the kids and her waitress job, she did what she could with the farm, and Manny did the rest. Or had until he'd had to return to Mexico. And this late in the year all her regular field hands had returned home also. Normally she and Manny could handle it together. But alone… She bit her lip. "I thought he would be back by now, but his mother took a turn for the worse."

"You should fire him."

"I can't." Manny had been her father's right hand man, and he'd become both her right and left hand man. He'd been the one constant on the farm. Or had been until two weeks ago. But Elisabeth understood what a commitment to family meant. "You don't fire someone because their mother is ill. He needs to be with her."

"What about your needs?" Kathy asked.

She needed someone to help her prepare the farm for winter. An extra pair of hands. Someone with two good arms and legs who could follow directions. It was already the beginning of October. Her stomach clenched. "I just need to find some temporary help." Temporary, cheap help.

"Where? And how are you going to pay them since you kept Manny on salary?"

Elisabeth could do the work alone, but she'd have to quit this job. Berry farming alone wouldn't support her family. She fought the panic rising in her throat.

Kathy squeezed her shoulder. "I'm worried about you, honey. You're too young to have to do all this on your own."

Elisabeth filled three glasses with ice and placed them on the tray. She had managed against the odds before; she would do it again this time. Tears stung her eyes, and she blinked them away. "I don't have a choice."

"You need a break." Kathy picked up the tray. "I'll take their orders and you deliver the food when you get back."

"Excuse me," a female voice said. Elisabeth turned and saw the stylishly dressed blonde from table four. The diamond ring on her finger could have fed a third world country for at least a year. And paid off the second mortgage on the farm and put at least two of her siblings through college. "I was wondering if you could bring a couple of slices of lime with the bottled water?"

"I'll take care of it, Miss." Kathy glanced at Elisabeth. "Get some fresh air."

She knew better than to argue with her boss, especially in front of a customer. And Elisabeth needed a few minutes alone. She stepped outside, took a deep breath and let the tears flow.

When Elisabeth returned to the kitchen, she was surprised to see Kathy and the customer from table four talking. The tray still sat on the counter, though limes had been added to the plate. As soon as they noticed her, they stopped chatting.

"Feel better after your break?" Kathy asked.

Elisabeth didn't allow herself the luxury of tears often because she was afraid once she started crying she wouldn't be able to stop. And this job was too important to let a pity party turn into a flood of tears. "Yes."

"You'll feel even better in a few minutes." Kathy picked up the pitcher and plate. "Elisabeth Wheeler, this is Cynthia Sterling. I do believe she's the answer to your prayers."

With that, Kathy left the kitchen. Elisabeth wasn't sure what was going on, but she knew the beautiful blond woman wearing designer clothes wasn't a guardian angel. And she'd stopped believing in fairy godmothers a long time ago.

Cynthia took a step toward her, and Elisabeth noticed her favoring her left foot. "When I came into the kitchen, I overheard you needed someone to help with your farm."

Elisabeth nodded. *Someone* about covered what she was looking for. As long as the person wasn't dangerous and a menace to society, she would hire him.

"I apologize for eavesdropping, but after you left, Kathy told me a little more about your situation. I'm sorry."

Elisabeth hated pity. She'd faced it from friends, neighbors, even strangers for too long.

"I want to help."

She wouldn't accept charity and that's the only way the beautiful blonde could help her. Elisabeth wiped the counter. "Thanks, but I don't see how you—"

"My friend, Henry, he's the one who was sitting across from my fiancé and I, needs a job. He's a good man, but made some bad investments and lost everything. He needs to turn his life around. Working on your farm would give him that chance."

She had to be kidding. Ralph Lauren Polo Country wasn't proper attire for *her* country. Cynthia's friend was dressed as if he was worth a million dollars with his leather jacket and lightly starched, perfectly pressed button-down shirt and knife-edge creased pants. "It's hard work. Manual work. Long hours outdoors."

"That's exactly what Henry loves to do. He's a get-your-hands-dirty type of guy."

Not the well-dressed guy at table four. Elizabeth appreciated Cynthia trying to help, but Henry was not what she needed. "No. I'm paying my foreman while he's away. I can't afford to pay another worker."

"I'll cover his expenses and his salary, say minimum wage."

Elisabeth managed to keep her jaw from dropping open. Henry would work on her farm and it wouldn't

"If Henry quits, you can keep the check. Deal?"

Instinct told her to take the check and take a chance on Henry. But Elisabeth didn't like taking chances on anyone. She didn't like opening herself and her family up to more disappointment. They'd all been hurt enough. Henry could cause trouble on all sorts of levels. She already knew he was a flirt.

But there was the money to consider. And the kids. And the farm. "I need the references."

Cynthia handed her the check, and Elisabeth stared at all the zeros. Ten thousand dollars. With that money…her pulse quickened.

"Here's a list of references." Cynthia gave her a cell phone and a small piece of paper. "Tell them Cynthia Sterling is setting Henry up for a little adventure of his own and ask whatever questions you might have."

"Don't I need Henry's last name?"

"It's Davenport, but his first name will suffice. You'll find out enough about Henry to make up your mind." She held on to her small purse. "If you don't want to hire Henry, simply return the check with my phone by the time we finish with lunch. If you will hire him, keep the check. Just give me your address and the time you get off work when you return my phone so we can drop him off."

"We could change our sleeping arrangements so Henry would have his own room." Elisabeth didn't know what prompted her to say the words. Sympathy? More like desperation.

"That would be perfect." Cynthia grinned. "Though I still think the barn would be fine."

As Elisabeth watched her limp back to the dining room, she clutched the check and prayed for good, solid reference checks. She hadn't had time for daydreams or fantasies in years, but today she wanted to believe in a guardian angel or fairy godmother or winning the lottery. Anything to justify what she wanted to do if Henry's references checked out.

And a part of Elisabeth thought they just might. Cynthia Sterling seemed like she could have a magic wand hidden somewhere on her.

Chapter Two

The food was better than Henry expected. And the service… Elisabeth with an *S* proved herself to be the world's best waitress. Whatever they wanted, as soon as they wanted. Nothing but polite words flowed from her smiling lips.

It was aggravating as hell.

Henry didn't want to see her, didn't want to hear her sweet voice. He wanted her to drop a plate, spill a drink, sneer at him. But she didn't. And he found it difficult—if not impossible—to keep from watching her every movement. He caught another glimpse of Elisabeth's support-hose-covered legs and felt a twinge in his groin.

Definitely time to get her out-of-sight and out-of-mind. "Let's get the check. Frank's waiting."

Frank was his long-time driver and would be driving them along the route Henry had mapped out. Wineries for tours and tastings, and dinner at a new restaurant in

Dundee. In a few short hours, the Berry Bistro would be nothing more than a memory. Back home in Portland, he would make seven different dates for next week. That would be enough to slam the door on the small-town waitress and make him forget she existed.

Elisabeth brought the check and returned Cynthia's cell phone, which she said had fallen out of her purse somehow. Cynthia grabbed the check. It was out of character for her to treat anyone to a meal, but Henry wasn't about to complain. She'd been so sweet to him during the entire lunch. Must be Cade's influence. A satisfied feeling settled over Henry, once again pleased his matchmaking skills were so attuned.

After the bill had been paid, he stood at the bistro's entrance. The temptation to glance back one last time was strong, but he was stronger. He walked out and slid into his limo.

The car moved forward, and relief washed over him. Someday he'd have a good laugh over his odd attraction to a waitress named Elisabeth in a tiny town called Berry Patch. But not today. An award-winning bottle of pinot noir had his name on it, and he couldn't wait for a sip.

Twenty minutes later, the limo stopped not at a winery, but at a Wal-Mart parking lot. "What's going on?" Henry asked.

"I'll be right back," Cynthia said. Several minutes later she returned with two large shopping bags and they were back on the road. Using Cade's Swiss Army knife, she cut the tags off an assortment of clothing items, placed her purchases in a large navy duffel bag and pushed it toward Henry's feet. "This is yours."

Henry furrowed his brow. "I'm confused."

"So am I," Cade said. "But these past few months I've

learned to sit back and relax and everything will work out fine."

"You've come so far." Cynthia kissed Cade's cheek. "And now it's Henry's turn. It's time to experience your own adventure. You'll see it's not all fun and games. And that you have to stop trying to control other people's lives."

"Can I help it if I know what's best for my friends?"

Cynthia tilted her chin. "I'm your friend so I must know what's best for you. Unless you're wrong about friends knowing what their friends need most."

She and Cade were living proof Henry knew what he was doing. Not to mention Brett and Laurel Matthews. It hurt Henry that Cynthia couldn't see that herself. "I'm not wrong."

"Then prove it. Go on an adventure. It's time to put your money where your mouth is."

Anticipation hung in the air. He glanced at Cade, who merely shrugged. Henry couldn't expect his friends to participate in his adventures if he wasn't willing to do the same. And this was Cynthia. She didn't know what he wanted or needed. She also knew nothing about planning an adventure. Challenging adventures took time and careful planning. Hers smacked of last minute. He could handle whatever she threw at him.

"Fine," Henry said finally. "I'll go on your little adventure and prove I'm right. That I know what's best for my friends. And when I win I get to plan your honeymoon."

Cade leaned forward. "Wait a minute."

"Don't worry, honey. We haven't gotten to the rewards yet." Cynthia assured him with confidence. "Your cell phone and wallet, please."

Henry handed them over. She removed his credit cards, his calling card and his cash before returning the wallet.

"It isn't safe to carry all these hundreds around." She gave him one twenty-dollar bill. "Here's the deal. You are still Henry Davenport, but the only money you have left in the world is this twenty. You are broke, out of work and homeless. You've been living off the generosity of your friends since making a string of bad investments."

Henry thought about his best friend, financial advisor and goddaughter's father, Brett Matthews. "Don't tell Brett."

Cynthia ignored him. "For the next month, you'll be working and living on a farm. You can only spend the money you earn."

"An entire month?" Henry asked.

"Or less if the foreman returns from Mexico. He may not want to keep you on."

Henry's knowledge of farms came from television shows. *Green Acres. Little House on the Prairie.* It wouldn't be that bad. Milk a cow or two. Feed some animals. Fix a broken fence. People pay good money to stay in the country and at dude ranches. This wasn't an adventure. It was a vacation. "What's the catch?"

"No catch," Cynthia said. "But if you spend any money you didn't earn or tell anyone the truth about yourself or return home before your time is up or get fired, you lose."

Sounded simple enough. "If I win?"

"If you last the entire month, I will never say another word about your adventures or matchmaking."

"And?" Henry always gave his friends rewards for participating in his adventures. Selecting the perfect prizes was half the fun.

"And the Smiling Moon Foundation's island camp will be named after you as well as our first born son."

Henry had donated the island where Cynthia and Cade spent their adventure to Cade's nonprofit foundation, but having it named Davenport would immortalize Henry. And if Cade and Cynthia named their child Henry, they would have to ask him to be the godfather. He loved being Noelle Matthews's godfather. She was so sweet and stared at him with such adoration and love. He wanted more godchildren to spoil. But most of all he wanted to prove he was right and Cynthia was wrong.

"And plan your honeymoon."

Cade frowned. "No."

"Yes," Cynthia said. "But if you lose the adventure, your birthday parties and legendary adventures come to an end."

Henry's heart fell to his feet. "I've already planned the next one."

"Then you had better stay on the farm for the entire time."

How hard could it be? If Cynthia could survive a deserted island, he could survive a farm. At least he'd have a roof over his head and indoor plumbing. "I'll do it."

Cynthia hit the intercom button. "To the farm, Frank."

Thirty minutes later, the limo passed a wooden sign that read Wheeler Berry Farm and turned left onto a gravel road. They passed a deserted fruit stand on one side of the road. The limo stopped in front of a metal building with large doors hanging open. The barn? Henry wasn't certain since barns were supposed to be red and constructed of wood and have animals living in them instead of rusted machinery and dirty farm equipment.

He stared at a two-story dilapidated farmhouse. He'd pictured a white picket fence, a swing on the porch and an older couple standing in the front yard. Not…this.

The house looked solid, but neglected. The anemic cream paint was cracked and peeling, and the green— or was it gray—door had seen better days. A plastic blue tarp covered half of the roof and fluttered in the breeze. One shutter hung haphazardly as if held by a single nail. At least there was a porch. Get rid of the flaking paint, add a swing and…it would still be bad.

A rooster cried out *cock-a-doodle-doo*. Henry thought they only did that at dawn.

"Having second thoughts?" Cynthia asked.

"No." He was up to seventeenth or eighteenth thoughts. But it was too late to back down. It wasn't as if he were going to live here forever. Only a month. Thirty days. Maybe thirty-one, but who was counting? He didn't see an outhouse, which must mean indoor plumbing. Or so he hoped. Henry swallowed. Hard.

Cynthia glanced at her watch. "We're a few minutes early. The farmer should be here shortly."

As if on cue, an ancient silver-and-black Suburban roared down the driveway, spewing a wake of gravel and dirt. Henry grabbed the blue duffel bag and exited the limo. He glanced at Frank, who had lowered his window. "Tell Brett to handle things while I'm away. Tell Laurel to take lots of pictures and video of Noelle. And in exactly one month, pick me up."

"Anything else, sir?"

"No." Henry stood next to Cynthia and watched the truck sputter to a stop next to them. The door opened, and he saw a foot. A foot wearing an ugly white shoe. Next came a support-hose-covered calf. "It can't be her."

"It is."

He'd known there had to be a catch. But not even Cynthia would… oh, yes, she would.

"And did I mention you'll be living with her, too?"

Elisabeth jumped down from the truck. She still wore her waitress outfit, but she'd removed her ponytail. Flowing blond hair surrounded her makeup-free face. She flipped her hair behind her shoulder and he felt as if he'd been sucker punched.

"Thank goodness you're not interested in her or it could be a really long month. We'll be going now." Cynthia waved to Elisabeth and gave Henry a peck on the cheek. "Have fun and be a good boy. You wouldn't want to be fired on your first day."

Before he knew it, the limo was heading down the long driveway toward the road, toward civilization. He watched the puff of dirt follow the limo until it disappeared. He stood alone. Cynthia's first mistake. Henry had sent his friends off in pairs. Of course, that was necessary to the matchmaking.

Unless Cynthia wanted Elisabeth to be his pair— his match.

An interesting thought. Too bad he wasn't up for a lifetime commitment with anyone. That just proved Cynthia didn't know him. But a month with Elisabeth, it wouldn't be so bad…. Who was he kidding? It couldn't get any worse.

The sound of another car door slamming, laughter and footsteps filled the still country air. Henry glanced at the Suburban. A little girl with blond ringlets ran around the front of the truck and latched on to Elisabeth's leg. Her megawatt grin lit up her small face.

Another girl, a few years older than the first, with gold wire-rimmed glasses and blond braids joined them. A sullen-looking, thin teenage boy wearing a black T-shirt with the faded words Trust No One on it shuffled his way around the truck and stood with his hands shoved in his faded jeans pockets. The defiance on his face matched the expression on his black T-shirt.

The trio of blond-haired females shared a striking resemblance. The boy had Elisabeth's blue eyes....

And that's when it hit Henry. It *was* worse. A lot worse.

Elisabeth didn't look old enough, but the proof was right in front of him. She had kids. His beautiful waitress was a mom. And just like brides, Henry didn't do moms.

Elisabeth's insides were coiled like a ball of string wrapped too tight. Any second she would unravel and fall apart. She placed her arm around Caitlin's shoulder. Holding her youngest sister's small, warm body gave Elisabeth a moment to regain her composure, a minute to draw an ounce of much-needed strength. Something told her she was going to need every bit of strength she could muster when it came to Henry Davenport.

His references had checked out. She'd heard enough about Henry not to worry about him murdering them in their sleep, but he was a pretty boy like her ex-fiancé Toby Cantrell, and pretty boys were never reliable. They always left when the going got tough.

Caitlin pointed toward Henry. "Who's that?"

"Caitlin Wheeler, meet Henry Davenport." Elisabeth tried to keep the corners of her mouth up. "Henry, this is my youngest sister, Caitlin."

As he made his way toward them, a dazzling grin broke over his handsome face. "Sister?"

Elisabeth nodded.

Caitlin extended her arm. "Hello."

He kissed the top of her hand and was rewarded with a giggle. "It's a pleasure to meet you."

"When I'm five I get to go to Disneyland." Caitlin tilted her head slightly. "Have you ever been to Disneyland?"

"I have," Henry said.

He kneeled, bringing him to Caitlin's level and closer to Elisabeth. Okay, he wasn't like her ex-fiancé, who never spoke to her siblings let alone acknowledged them. But Henry was still a charmer. His nearness disturbed her, made her feel warm and uncomfortable. She wanted to step back, but she wasn't about to leave Caitlin's side. Elisabeth bit the inside of her cheek.

"Disneyland is one of my favorite places in the world."

Caitlin moved closer to him. A surprise since she was usually shy around strangers. For the first ten minutes, that was. "Do you know Minnie Mouse? I want to see Minnie and Cinderella and Ariel and Jasmine and Sleeping Beauty…."

"What about Snow White?" Henry asked.

Caitlin nodded. "And the seven drawers."

"Dwarfs," Elisabeth corrected.

"Dwarfs," Caitlin repeated. "Oh, and I want to see Belle, too. I want to be five."

"How old are you?" Henry asked.

She raised her fingers. "Four. How old are you?"

"Caitlin," Elisabeth whispered. "It's not polite to ask someone for their age."

"He asked me."

"I did." Henry's eyes sparkled with laughter. "I'm thirty-four."

Elisabeth did a double take. He looked younger. Not that thirty-four was old. She would be twenty-five in a few months. But she felt much older.

"Do you like ballerinas and princesses?" Caitlin asked.

"I do," Henry admitted. "Do you think you could help me with something?"

Wide-eyed, Caitlin nodded. Elisabeth placed her hands on her sister's thin shoulders.

"I have a goddaughter named Noelle." Henry's smile softened as he spoke the name. "She'll turn one on Christmas day, but I'm guessing she'll like ballerinas and princesses when she's your age. Do you think you could show me the kind of toys and dress-up clothes she would like so I can be prepared?"

Caitlin grabbed his hand. "Let's go to my room."

"I don't think so." Elisabeth wasn't about to let a stranger be alone with her baby sister or with any of her siblings. "Henry needs to get settled in Sam's room."

"Where's Sam going to sleep?" Caitlin asked.

"In your bed."

Caitlin frowned. "Where will I sleep?"

"With me."

"I'll go move my babies and animals." She skipped to the porch, bounced up the stairs and jumped inside the house.

"Cute girl," Henry said.

With blond ringlets and big, sparkling blue eyes, Caitlin was the definition of cute and knew it, too. Elisabeth nodded. "But she'll talk your ear off. From the time she wakes up until after she's supposed to be asleep, she talks. I was so worried when she turned two and only said a few words, but in a couple of months those words turned into sentences and conversations. She's quite the linguist now."

Elisabeth babbled worse than her stylist while she cut hair. She was just tired and hungry after today's shift at the café—make that bistro. That would explain why Elisabeth felt off-center and a little dizzy. She'd been up before the sun and her day was far from over.

Sam, eleven and perpetually bored, stepped forward. "So you want to work here?"

"I'm Henry Davenport." He extended his hand. "You're Elisabeth's...brother?"

"Sam Wheeler." He shook Henry's hand, but distrust echoed in his voice. Sam acted like a dog having his territory invaded. Manny might run the farm, but ever since their parents' deaths almost four years ago, Sam had been the man of the house. He took the job seriously. He straightened his narrow shoulders and puffed out what little chest he had. "You know anything about farming, Mr. Davenport?"

"Sam," Elisabeth cautioned. She needed to work on the children's manners. Not to mention a million other things. How did women make it as mothers? It was going on four years and she still hadn't figured it out.

"It's okay." Henry met Sam's wary gaze. "First, call me Henry. My father was Mr. Davenport. And second, I don't know much about farming."

Sam shot her a why-is-he-here look. Elisabeth felt the same way. Henry might not be qualified, but he looked strong and healthy. All his bones seemed to be intact, and he was breathing. And there was the ten thousand dollar check that came with him. The rest would…follow.

Henry smiled. "Don't worry, Sam, I'm a fast learner. I graduated from Harvard."

"Harvard?" Eight-year-old child prodigy, Abby, perked up. "Do you think you got your money's worth from a Harvard education? After all if you amortized the cost difference between a state university and an Ivy League college and added in an—"

"That's enough for now, Abigail." Elisabeth tugged on Abby's braid and hoped their financial situation changed by the time her sister was ready for college. At this point none of them would be able to attend without scholarships and financial aid. "You'll have plenty of time to discuss higher education options later." Elisabeth turned her attention to Henry. "Abby's what you might call gifted."

"She's a freakin' genius," Sam added.

Elisabeth sighed. "Why don't you two go check on Caitlin?"

For once, they both did as told. About time. Elisabeth rubbed her lower back.

She stared at Henry's face, unable to find any fault with what she saw. He wasn't so much a pretty boy as a classically handsome man. Okay, he was totally gorgeous if she wanted to be honest with herself. Which she didn't, Elisabeth realized with a start. Every instinct screamed to keep her distance.

A mischievous glint shone in Henry's eyes.

"You're good with children." The words tumbled out of her mouth. Had he realized she was staring? Probably. He'll think she liked him. Unfamiliar warmth flooded her cheeks. Great. Now she *was* blushing. This wouldn't do. So he was good-looking. She could handle it. Elisabeth squared her shoulders. "Do you have any children of your own?"

"No," he answered quickly. "I don't plan on having any. Kids are too much work."

"But there are lots of rewards."

"I know. Parenthood is wonderful for many people," he said. "But not me."

She didn't like that. Nor did she get it. He seemed a natural with Caitlin. "Why not?"

"I'm not father material," Henry admitted. "Too much responsibility. Someone always counting on you to be there or do something for them. I like to have too much fun."

He sounded like Toby, a large child living inside a man's body. *Kids only get in the way. We'll be living our lives for them, not ourselves.* She hated to call the job off when she needed the money so badly, but not even for ten thousand dollars would she subject the kids to someone who didn't like them. Elisabeth stiffened. "If you don't like kids, this may not be the job for you."

"I like kids provided they aren't my own."

She reminded herself he wasn't here forever. Only until Manny returned. "Welcome to Wheeler Berry Farm. We haven't been formally introduced. I'm Elisabeth Wheeler."

"Henry Davenport, but you already knew that."

His perfectly straight teeth flashed in a brilliant smile reminding Elisabeth that Sam's braces were coming up. "Cynthia told me your name so I could check your references."

His eyes widened. "You checked my...references?"

"Of course I did. I'm not in the habit of hiring people this way, but I know enough to check references," Elisabeth admitted. "Manny, my foreman, usually takes care of it. But his mother is ill and he needs to be with her. That's why I needed help. The kids and I can't do it ourselves."

"How old are the kids?"

"Sam's eleven, Abigail's eight and Caitlin's four. They're good kids. Most of the time. Okay, some of the time. They have their moments. Will you be able to handle that?"

"Yes."

He wet his lips, and she had to force her gaze away from them. Strange. She wasn't in the habit of staring at men's lips and wondering how it would be to kiss them.

"What about your parents?" he asked.

Sadness washed over her. No one had asked about them in so long. Everyone in Berry Patch knew what had happened. No one wanted to bring it up, no one except the state caseworker who checked in on her siblings.

"They're gone." Elisabeth met his inquisitive gaze. She didn't want to talk about them. "Your references gave glowing recommendations. One person, Brett Matthews, seemed surprised by your...situation." That was putting it mildly, but she didn't want to hurt Henry's feelings. "I hope I didn't cause any problems for you."

"You didn't. Brett is a financial advisor," Henry said. "He must have assumed I was following his advice."

That made sense. But Brett had recommended Henry for the job, saying he was loyal with a heart of gold and would be a helpful employee. He added Henry was good with children and baby-sat Brett's nine-month-old daughter occasionally. That, in addition to the ten thousand dollar check from Cynthia Sterling, had sealed the deal in Elisabeth's mind.

Geese flew overhead. One more sign autumn had arrived, and it was time to prepare for winter. Good thing she'd found help.

"Tell me about your farm."

"I'm the fifth generation of Wheelers to farm this land. We have over a hundred acres of the most fertile land in the Willamette Valley. Some of the original homestead was sold off during the Depression." She had a love-hate relationship with the land, but pride filled her voice. She hadn't succeeded, but she hadn't failed, either. This might not have been her dream growing up, but it was her life now. One she wasn't about to let go. No matter how difficult things got, she would make sure the farm thrived for her sisters and brother. They would always have a home to come back to when they got older. "Thirty acres are row crops—beans and corn. The others are berries—raspberries, marionberries, boysenberries and evergreen blackberries. We have a small vegetable and herb garden and a handful of livestock. A horse, a cow, a few goats and some chickens."

"As I told Sam, I've never worked on a farm before."

He sounded sincere, honest. Maybe this was going to work out. Elisabeth hoped so. "Cynthia explained that to me, but I will show you what to do. And I'll be here to answer any questions. That is, when I'm not working at the restaurant."

"Sounds like you keep busy."

"I do."

"What do you do for fun?"

Fun? That word hadn't been part of her vocabulary for years. Yet with Henry standing right next to her with a devastating grin on his face, she could imagine having fun with him. A lot of fun. The thought made her wish he wasn't going to be living here for the next month. "I—"

The slamming of the screen door interrupted her. Sam stood on the porch scowling. "Caitlin's on the pot and needs you."

"Be right there." Relieved for the interruption, Elisabeth brushed a strand of hair off her face. "That's my cue to go inside."

Chapter Three

Standing on the porch with his duffel bag slung over his shoulder, Henry steeled himself for what lay on the other side of the torn screen door. He wasn't expecting the Ritz, but he didn't relish the thought of living in a dive for the next month. On rare occasions, he had stayed in four-star hotels, but didn't like roughing it. He hoped for clean and comfortable. Perhaps it would have a rustic, lodge-like charm.

As Elisabeth opened the door, it squeaked. Forest-green paint peeled away revealing various layers of blue, yellow and orange. "My great-grandfather built this house."

Henry respected being surrounded by so much history and family. His own grandfather had left him a legacy. Instead of a farm though, Henry had received a multi-million dollar trust fund that Brett Matthews had turned into billions. Henry was happy old Gramps had been a businessman and not a farmer. Without his money, Henry couldn't imagine what he would do every day.

"It was a wedding present for my great-grandmother."

"How romantic," Henry said.

The faraway look in Elisabeth's eyes intrigued him. "I suppose it was."

She motioned him inside. As he passed her, a floral scent, wildflowers, wafted in the air. The fragrance was subtle, too light for a perfume, and he wondered if it was her soap or shampoo. As he was contemplating whether she preferred a bubble bath or a shower and what she might look like taking one, she bumped into him. "I'm sorry."

"My fault," he said, turning. She was soft in all the right places. His temperature shot up. "I was blocking the doorway."

They stood mere inches away from each other. A second passed, then another. He should move out of her way.

Or step aside.

Or kiss her.

"Excuse me," she said finally and pushed past him.

So much for his being suave and debonair. This wasn't like him at all. Must be the country air interfering with his gift of charm and sophistication.

As he followed her into the living room, the scent of apples and cinnamon lingered in the air, making his mouth water. The delicious fragrance appealed to both his nose and his stomach.

"I need to help Caitlin. I'll be right back." She hurried up the stairs before he could say anything.

Henry stood in the living room. His first thought was that a tornado had hit the place. But he realized the house didn't look sturdy enough to withstand gale-force winds. That meant the mess was most likely man-made. Or rather kid-made.

He glanced around. How could three kids do so much damage?

Old stuffed animals that looked like thrift store rejects sat on the couch. Bent and ripped playing cards were scattered over the scratched hardwood floors. Coloring books and crayons covered the beat-up and ring-stained coffee table. Overturned chairs were haphazardly covered with blankets and pillows. A stack of newspapers littered a recliner.

The papers moved. Henry jumped back.

A fat, gray, long-haired cat burrowed from underneath the pile of newspapers. Its hypnotic green eyes focused on Henry, then it turned, stuck its rear and fluffy tail in the air and bounded up the stairs. Henry wished he could walk out the front door and back home.

Elisabeth returned sooner than he expected. "The house is always a mess. I try to get everybody to pick up after themselves, but there's only so much one can do."

"It has that…lived-in look."

"Lived-in." She smiled. "You're just being polite, but I like it."

I like you.

"You'll see how lived-in things get with kids around."

Henry slammed the brakes on his feelings for Elisabeth. He understood his physical attraction to her. Beautiful, gorgeous, sexy, she was all those things and more, but he didn't understand why the rest of the package—waitress with a farm and three siblings—wasn't putting a damper on said attraction.

Sure they weren't her kids, but with her parents gone, they might as well be. And he avoided dating women with children. He was worried about an innocent by-stander getting hurt once whatever relationship he was involved in came to an end. And they always came to an end. He couldn't help himself.

A good reason to keep his distance from his appealing boss. As much distance as possible considering he was living in the same house and working on the farm with her. No matter his attraction, it couldn't go further. There would be no flirting between him and Elisabeth with an *S*. Regret inched its way down his spine.

"This is the living room," she said, looking away. "We have a brand new TV-VCR combo, but no satellite dish. We have a few videos. Though there isn't much time to sit around and watch television."

The set was small—nineteen inches if he was being generous.

"The kids were so excited when we won it at Peterson's Electronics and Hardware store last month." They weren't the only ones. As Elisabeth smiled, a dimple appeared on her left cheek and made him rethink his no-mom rule, but only for a moment.

So much excitement for a run-of-the-mill television set. He'd been excited by his theater room back home with its McIntosh sound system and high-definition plasma display for a couple of days until the novelty wore off, as it did with his other must-have toys. "How did you win it?"

"We guessed the number of nails in a five-gallon water bottle. Abby figured it out. She was off by four. No one else was close." Elisabeth lowered her voice. "She's good with numbers. And pretty much anything else."

"What about Sam?" Henry followed her through a doorway and into a large kitchen. The white cupboards brightened the room and made up for the faded, peel-ing floral wallpaper. On the floor sat different shaped bowls. No doubt the gray cat wasn't the only pet.

"Sam's a big help with the girls and the farm," she said. "But I don't want him to grow up too fast. He should be a kid for as long as possible."

The kitchen was a mess, too, with bowls and glasses covering the faux-wood Formica countertops. Breakfast dishes? He could only hope. The one pleasant item he saw was a pie on the stove. Must be what he smelled earlier.

"Help yourself to whatever's in the cupboards or fridge. I keep the cookie jar filled, but with the kids you never know how many will be left." She motioned to a large ceramic bowl filled with apples, oranges and ba-nanas. "You're welcome to join us for meals. It's never anything fancy, but food is food."

His personal chef would beg to differ, but Henry wasn't about to tell her that. "Thank you."

Her gaze met his. "You might want to wait until you taste my cooking before you thank me."

"I'll take my chances."

A twinge of pink colored her cheeks. He didn't know many women who still blushed. He liked it.

"The kids are a little too quiet," she said. "We'd bet-ter head upstairs."

The staircase was wide with a wood banister and carved balustrades. Photographs covered the wall lead-ing up to the second floor. A picture of Sam riding a tri-cycle. Abby sitting on the back of a pony. Caitlin in the center of a pumpkin patch. Henry did a double take. "You were a cheerleader?"

"In high school."

"Homecoming queen, too?"

"No, but I was the Berry Patch Harvest Princess."

"Sounds better than homecoming queen."

"It was." Her smile reached her eyes. The effect—stunning. "I got to wear a crown for an entire week and ride on a float."

"That does beat homecoming queen. But what is the Berry Patch Harvest and why do they need a princess?"

"Every year, Berry Patch hosts a big harvest festival. It's a glorified country fair with a carnival, dance, food and competitions."

Henry had never been to a country fair. It sounded old-fashioned, but fun. Maybe that would be a good theme for one of his birthday parties, though he didn't know what kind of adventure would go along with a fair. "Will you be running for the title again this year?"

"I'm too old for that."

He wasn't sure of her age. She looked to be in her mid-to-late twenties. "I doubt that."

"Twenty-one is too old to enter."

"That's too bad, because I bet you were the best Harvest Princess Berry Patch ever had."

The corners of her mouth curved. She started to speak, but stopped. Henry thought he saw gratitude in her eyes.

"There are three bedrooms and—" she pushed open a door "—a bathroom up here."

"Bathroom?"

"There's only one in the house."

But it was in the house. No treks to the outhouse in the middle of the night. He pumped his fist at his side. Cynthia would be so disappointed.

"It's large, though, with both a shower and a bathtub."

"Abby and I fit in there," Caitlin whispered from a doorway. A small baby doll was tucked under her left arm.

Henry wondered if he and Elisabeth would fit. He stared at the little girl. Erase that thought.

"Why are you being so quiet?" Elisabeth asked.

"All of my babies are sleeping in my new bed. Your bed." Caitlin put her finger to her lips and made a shushing sound. "We don't want to wake them. Do you want to be the daddy?"

Henry's jaw tensed. "Uh, not right now."

"Later?"

"Where's Abby?" Elisabeth whispered, trying to let Henry off the hot seat.

"With Sam."

She took the little girl's right hand. "Help me show Henry to his room."

As they walked down the hallway, Elisabeth pointed out her room. It was on the same side of the house as the bathroom. Henry could sneak into her bedroom by feigning to have entered the wrong door on the way to the bathroom. Thinking this way was a natural reflex, and he would have to stop.

A month-long fling might be nice, but not with the children around. Besides if he fell for Elisabeth, he would prove Cynthia knew what was best for him. She didn't. No one did. No one knew what he needed period. Not that it mattered. It was just the way things were. And had always been from the time he was a child. Henry shook aside the memories creeping into his mind.

He had to concentrate on the adventure and focus. He was here to be a farmer, not a lover. Elisabeth might not be a teenager, but innocence shone in her eyes. This was a woman who would expect a commitment. And that was something Henry wouldn't make to anyone.

Marriage was to be avoided at all costs. His father had said the same thing about love. That was one piece of advice Henry had listened to. There would never be another Mrs. Davenport. His mother had been the last in a long line of power-driven, wealth-seeking, social-climbing women who married for the money-rich, love-poor life of a Davenport.

"And this—" Elisabeth stopped in front of a door with an Enter at your own Risk sign on it "—will be your room."

The door opened. Abby sat at a desk; at least Henry assumed underneath all the papers and clothes was some sort of furniture, and stacked a jumble of comic books.

"Hello," she said, then returned to the task at hand.

"Samuel Joseph Wheeler," Elisabeth said. "I told you to clean your room."

"It's cleaner than it was."

Henry gulped. He couldn't imagine what it had been like before. The after picture was bad enough. It made the living room seem immaculate. Stuff was everywhere. Piles, stacks, clutter, you name it. Forget about looking lived-in. Messy described Sam's room perfectly. Disaster area worked, too. But Henry doubted any element of Mother Nature could be responsible for this amount of chaos. It probably qualified for the Federal Disaster Relief Fund.

Elisabeth gathered pieces of paper from the floor. "I'll be back after dinner to straighten it up."

Forget about straightening. It would take a dump truck to clean this place. There was a clear space from the door to the bed, and the only flat surface not covered with junk were the metal-frame bunk beds.

Elisabeth continued to clean. "You should be so ashamed by the condition of this room, Sam."

"It's not that bad." Sam climbed onto the top bunk. "Better than the pink girlie-girl room I have to stay in."

"I like pink," Caitlin said.

Pink would be better than this. Lace curtains and baby dolls would be better than this. Think of the bright side, he told himself. No need to pick up after yourself. One thing like home.

"Oh, yeah." Sam pointed to a four-foot-high vertical column with clothes hanging off the top and out the sides like a multicolored cascading fountain. "I cleaned out a drawer for you to use."

So that was a dresser and not an abstract work of textiles and wood. Imagine that.

"We don't have a guest room," Elisabeth said.

"There's always the barn," Sam added and earned a glare from his big sister.

"It's fine." No matter how Henry felt about his accommodations, he didn't want to hurt Elisabeth's feelings. It wasn't her fault he'd underestimated Cynthia Sterling. This was turning out to be more of an adventure than he ever thought it would be. He noticed Elisabeth's forehead creased with worry. She didn't seem to care that was how wrinkles formed. "Really."

She smiled, and a warm feeling wrapped itself around Henry's heart. "Why don't you get unpacked while I fix dinner?"

A home-cooked meal. That would be a great way to end the first day of his adventure. And if dessert turned out to be the pie in the kitchen with a scoop of vanilla ice cream...oh, man. He couldn't wait. Whether he liked it or not, Elisabeth with her pretty face and luscious body had wormed her way under his skin. He hoped her cooking would do the same with his stomach and take his mind off the rest of her. "What's for dinner?"

"Macaroni and cheese with hamburger."

"My favorite," Caitlin cried.

He searched for a polite word to describe the horrific thought running through his brain. "What a combo."

His stomach agreed and launched an immediate protest. Henry had never eaten macaroni and cheese, unless he counted fettuccine Alfredo. Wasn't it orange and didn't it come out of a box? He couldn't fathom how to eat that with a hamburger. Wouldn't a bun and macaroni be overkill on the grains?

"I'll be sure to make enough for seconds," Elisabeth said.

"Great." Henry forced a smiled. Maybe they delivered pizza out in the sticks. He did have twenty dollars.

Henry couldn't remember the last time he'd unpacked his own bag. He attempted to fold a white T-shirt the way his housekeeper folded them at home. On the third try, he gave up and shoved it in the drawer as best as he could. Reaching for another T-shirt, he felt as if he were being watched. He turned and saw three pairs of blue eyes fixated on him. Sam's gaze was intense. Abby's inquisitive. Caitlin's playful.

Attention had always been a good thing. Until now.

Henry was used to little kids, Caitlin's age and younger. Babies, not big kids. He'd never met a female he couldn't charm, so the two girls weren't going to be problems, but the boy would be another story. Henry picked up the forest-green T-shirt and took a shot at being friendly anyway. "Seen any good movies?"

Sam tossed a small rubber ball against the wall. "Nope."

"What's a movie?" Caitlin asked.

"It's like a video except you pay for a ticket and watch it on a big screen in a theater and eat popcorn," Abby explained.

Caitlin grinned. "I like popcorn."

"So do I," Henry said. "You don't go to the movies?"

"There aren't any theaters in Berry Patch," Abby answered.

Sam frowned. "There's nothing in Berry Patch."

Thump, thump, thump. The sound of Sam's ball against the hardwood floor reminded Henry of a bloated metronome. The bouncing continued, as did the staring. He didn't attempt to fold the next shirt and tossed it into the drawer. The sooner he finished unpacking, the better. Next out of the duffel bag was a pair of white briefs.

"Wearing boxers is better for your sperm count," Abby said.

The thumping of Sam's ball stopped. Henry glanced at the young girl. "Excuse me?"

She adjusted her gold wire-rimmed glasses. "Wearing briefs can have an adverse effect on a man's sperm count as does riding a bike. The temperature increases and—"

"Thanks for the warning. I'll keep that in mind next time I'm shopping." Even though his top button was undone, his collar felt two sizes too tight. No man wanted to discuss his sperm count but especially not with an eight-year-old. He grabbed the rest of his clothes from the duffel bag and dumped them into the drawer. "All done."

"At least he's not a neat freak," Sam muttered. Another throw and the ball bounced across the floor to Henry's feet.

He grabbed it. "Anyone want to go downstairs?"

No one said anything so he tossed the ball back to Sam and headed to the stairs. Halfway down, Henry realized he was being followed. He continued into the living room. The sofa was clean so he sat. Abby sat on one side of him; Caitlin plopped down on the other. Sam stood, glaring.

Elisabeth entered from the kitchen. "It's time to feed the animals."

Sam groaned. "Do we have to?"

"No chores, no dessert."

As she stepped aside, the kids stampeded into the kitchen. The slamming of a door told Henry they were gone. Thank goodness. A moment of peace and no one watching him. Except Elisabeth.

"I hope they didn't bother you too much," she said.

A police interrogation would have been easier. Henry wondered if he should mention Abby's comment about briefs and sperm count, but thought better of it. He didn't want to worry Elisabeth. "I'll get used it."

"I'm sure you will." She wiped her hands on her pants. She'd changed out of her uniform and into a pair of worn-in-all-the-right-places jeans and a white T-shirt. Simple, yet stylish. He imagined her in a French maid's outfit with a feather duster in her hand. This time his pants felt tight, not his collar. "Would you like to see the crops?" she asked.

Over the years, women had asked him to see a variety of things, but crops had never been one of them. Until today he'd never thought about what a crop would look like. Now he would be working in them. Or was that with them? "Seeing the crops would be great."

She led him through the kitchen. Non-matching pots and pans covered the stove, but the counter was now clean. He noticed a black-and-white cow cookie jar in the corner. "We don't have much time before dinner, but you can see a little before it gets too dark."

He stepped out the back door. A grassy area surrounded the house and a rusted swing set took up one corner. It looked more like a death trap than play equipment and made him wonder if the kids had had tetanus shots. A garden lay to the right, and beyond that row after row of crops. The knee-high bushes were tied together. Berries, he assumed. They might be beans. At least it wasn't corn. He knew what corn plants looked like.

"These are marionberries," Elisabeth explained. "We harvest half our berry acres each year. The others are cut down to the ground to strengthen the roots as they grow back. You'll be helping me train them."

"Train them?" Henry asked. "Do they do tricks?"

She stared at him without the hint of a smile on her face. He didn't get it. He was being his adorable, charming self, but wasn't impressing her one bit.

Elisabeth pulled back the leaves to show him the inside of the bush. "Cane berries are trained to grow on trellises."

"Like grapes," he said.

"Exactly."

See, he wasn't without farming knowledge. Wine and champagne he knew something about. "There's a…" He was about to tell her about the château and vineyard where he stayed in France last year. Instead he pointed to the stack of white boxes amid the berry plants. "What is that?"

"Beehives. We usually don't have them this late in

the year, but the beekeeper hasn't picked up the remaining ones. We rent hives each spring for the fields to help with pollination so the blooms turn into berries. It's extra insurance for harvest time."

"You don't take any chances."

"We can't afford to." As their gazes met, he felt a tug on his heart. Must be her eyes. He was a sucker for baby blues. "I hope you realize what you've gotten yourself into. We have to be prepared for winter. When the weather is good we put in long hours. It's hard work."

"I can handle it." Henry could handle anything for a month. So he got a little dirty. He'd think of it as a poor man's mud bath. Nothing like the ones he'd taken in Calistoga, but he would survive. And the manual work would be good for him. With no access to a gym out here he needed some type of workout. And he liked being outside. Not a bad gig after all.

Elisabeth raised a brow. He didn't blame her for having doubts. She knew nothing about him. He looked forward to surprising her with his innate abilities.

"Besides training the canes, you'll be moving the irrigation equipment. We also need to keep the grass short between the rows of berries so you'll be mowing. We use a tractor to pull the mower. Will that be a problem?"

His mouth nearly gaped. "I get to drive a tractor?"

She nodded. "Do you like to drive?"

Henry pictured himself behind the wheel of a large, shiny, brand-spanking-new John Deere with a baseball cap on and grinned. He wouldn't have to worry about missing his Porsche and Hummer while he was here. "I love to drive."

"Good. We have lots of vehicles to drive around here—trucks, tractors. We also use four-wheelers,

ATVs, to get around. Saves a lot of time since there's so much land to cover." Elisabeth stopped at a dirt path dividing the marionberries from another type of berry. "We also use the dirt roads to get equipment in and out."

He couldn't imagine what the equipment might be, but he didn't care. Talk about getting lucky. He was getting paid to drive farm machinery and ATVs. Maybe he should have gotten a job before. This wasn't going to be work; this was going to be fun.

"You'll also be spraying. Timing is critical during bloom time, but not so much now. We spray before the rain hits to keep the berries from molding."

"I can't wait." And Henry couldn't. This was sounding better by the minute. Working heavy machinery was a dream come true. Now if he could get a little chummier with Elisabeth.

Sam chased a screaming Caitlin out of the barn.

Strike that. No chumming allowed.

"We should head back inside," she said. "I need to finish cooking."

"Anything I can do to help?" He never did his own cooking but the least he could do was offer. No one would ever accuse him of not having proper manners.

"Thanks, but I've got it under control."

Just like everything else, Henry realized. His respect for her increased a notch. He wouldn't want her job for anything. The responsibility and commitment. Talk about overwhelming. Just the thought made him shudder. He'd stick to planning birthday parties and adventures and matchmaking his friends. Things he knew how to do and did well.

He followed her into the kitchen. The aroma made his stomach take notice. "Smells good."

"Tastes even better."

Henry's eyes locked on her mouth, on her full lips. They were unpainted and more beautiful than those of a supermodel. And he'd kissed many a supermodel in his days. He couldn't help but wonder what kissing Elisabeth would feel like. He shouldn't want a taste, but he did.

Chapter Four

Dinner was over. Not an ounce of Elisabeth's macaroni and cheese with hamburger meat and tomatoes remained. Henry had helped himself to three servings and kept saying how delicious it was. Funny, but the way he acted made her think he'd never tasted macaroni and cheese before. At least he enjoyed it, and that pleased her. More than it should.

As she dished up berry pie à la mode, tonight seemed like a typical Saturday night. The air vibrated with giggles and singing. Arguments erupted from the table behind her. Things seemed so normal until she glanced back and saw Henry.

Nothing was normal this evening. Nor would it be with Henry Davenport here. She was as certain of that as rain falling in Oregon's wine country during the month of July.

She placed his dessert in front of him and passed out the other plates.

"We have a tradition that my daddy started," Abby explained. "On Saturdays we take turns telling everyone our favorite thing that happened during the week."

"You do this every Saturday?" Henry asked.

Sam rolled his eyes. "Not only on Saturdays."

"Weekdays, we talk about how our day went," Abby explained. "On Sundays, we say what we are thankful for."

Elisabeth glanced over at Henry. "You don't have to participate."

"I want to."

He smiled, one of the most dazzling, genuine smiles she'd ever seen in her life. Elisabeth felt lightheaded. She must be more tired than she realized. That was the only explanation for her reaction. She sat, vowing to get more sleep tonight. "Whose turn to start?"

"Mine." Caitlin placed her spoon on her plate. "My favorite thing was the tea party I had with my baby dolls and Sam. We ate cookies and drank iced tea. I like when we have real food. Sam does, too."

"Only if it's cookies." Sam's face was Roma tomato red. Elisabeth was tempted to thank him for playing with Caitlin, but he looked too embarrassed as it was. No need to rub it in. She could talk with him later in private.

"You're lucky to have such a nice big brother, Caitlin." Henry scooped up another bite of pie and ice cream. "I don't have any brothers or sisters to play with."

Sam squirmed in his seat. "I just did it for the cookies, sheesh."

"You can come to my next tea party." Two lines appeared above Caitlin's button nose. "Sam, is it okay if he comes?"

Sam shrugged. "Whatever. As long as there are enough cookies for me."

He focused a little too hard on the dessert in front of him. Trying to play it cool in front of Henry. Maybe having another male around would be good for Sam.

"I'm looking forward to it." Henry smiled at Sam. "Like you, I'm always up for cookies. Especially chocolate chip."

The sincere tone of his voice made Elisabeth believe he was being honest. Sam stopped shifting in his chair so he must have believed Henry, too.

For a man who didn't think he was father material, he sure had a way with kids. And it wasn't only that. She'd never met anyone like Henry. Nothing seemed to faze him. Oh, that grin of his faltered when he saw Sam's room, but within seconds it was back. He seemed to enjoy whatever life threw at him. At least he had so far. Tomorrow when he had to work might be a different story.

"You're next, Sam," Abby said, then shoved a spoonful of ice cream into her mouth.

"My favorite thing was seeing Aaron's skateboarding accident. Blood was everywhere." Sam mimicked the crash. "It was so cool."

Boys. Elisabeth grimaced. Maybe if she were eleven…she didn't think so. "No one repeat this to Aaron, okay?"

Everyone nodded.

"It's my turn," Henry said. "My favorite thing was when I met a nice family who lives on a farm in Berry Patch."

"Do we know them?" Caitlin asked.

"He means us, dorkface," Sam muttered.

Elisabeth narrowed her eyes. "Language, Samuel."

He nodded.

"I'm happy to be here and I can't wait to get to know all of you." Henry looked at each of the kids, then his gaze rested upon Elisabeth.

Especially you.

She thought he'd said the words out loud, but realized his mouth hadn't spoken them, his eyes had. She wanted to look away, but couldn't. She'd never felt anything like it, not even with Toby, and she wasn't certain if she wanted to feel it ever again. Uncertain, excited, nervous. Her emotions were as varied as the lunch menu at the bistro.

Heat spread through her. A burning heat, and she didn't like it. She took a bite of ice cream. Not that one spoonful would help. She was going to need the entire half gallon to cool herself down.

And once she cooled down she could not allow this to happen again. She would have to be careful where Henry was concerned. Her life wasn't her own. She had no time for romance or fanciful thoughts. No time to chase her own dreams. Her responsibility was to the children and the farm. It's what her parents would have wanted and expected. So why was the truth suddenly so disappointing?

"I'm next." Abby's eyes danced with excitement. "My favorite thing was being the second person picked for Madison Patrick's team. I was the right fielder for most of the game, but I got to pitch at the end and struck Danielle McLean out."

"That's great." Elisabeth forgot about her own troubles and clapped her hands together. "Now tell us everything that happened. Don't leave out any details."

As Abby described the game and events leading up to it, Elisabeth relished her sister's success. Abby's biggest wish was for her athletic ability to match her intellectual ability. She wasn't the most coordinated kid, but she gave everything her all. Some kids didn't care about that. To them, Abigail Wheeler was simply the class brain with glasses and the last one to be picked for a team, any team.

"Why didn't you tell us before?" Elisabeth asked.

"I wanted to save it for tonight." Abby grinned. "You're next."

"Let's see." Elisabeth was tempted to say finding Henry, but she didn't want to give him the wrong impression. Not that he thought that way about her. Still, she couldn't forget how he had stared at her a few minutes ago. Her pulse raced thinking about it. That was warning enough. Henry should not be her favorite thing. She had to remember what was most important—her brother and sisters. Toby had said no man would want all the extra baggage she brought into a relationship. And so far, he'd been right. But Elisabeth didn't care. She wanted her siblings and loved them more than anything. And would continue to do so.

Henry might say he loved children so long as they weren't his and be charming to them, but the charm would fade. And he would leave. At least the kids hadn't really liked Toby.

"My favorite thing happened tonight," she said, finally. "It was sitting here listening to all of you."

Sam groaned. "You always say that."

"But it's the truth." And it was. More than anything, Elisabeth wanted to make this a happy home for her brother and sisters. Nothing gave her more pleasure than listening to their favorite things, even if it turned out to be seeing Aaron Eliot's blood.

"And sweet." The look in Henry's eyes was anything but sugary and sweet. "Just like you."

"And the pie," Caitlin added.

He laughed. The deep, rich sound rumbled its way straight to Elisabeth's heart. Forget about more ice cream. She needed a tall glass of water with lots of ice. He winked at her. Her blood started to boil. Make that a pitcher or better yet, a water tower full.

Water wasn't Henry's normal nightcap, but it was better than juice. Or milk. With a glass in hand, he went into the living room.

Saturday night on the farm. Quiet, peaceful, boring. One night of this would be fine. But thirty? Forget it. Somehow he would have to liven things up.

Not only for him, but Elisabeth. She'd been cleaning ever since the kids went to bed. First the dishes—by hand because they had no dishwasher—then the kitchen, now the living room.

He wasn't sure how he could help her—his housekeeper cleaned for him—but Elisabeth was paying him to work, not sit around. "Do you want some help?" Henry asked.

"I'm almost done, but thanks." She folded a pastel rainbow-colored Afghan and laid it over the back of the couch. "You should relax. Get used to being here. After tonight you'll have a lot of work to do."

He didn't consider driving a tractor work, but he appreciated the hospitality. She had gone out of her way to make him feel welcome. In spite of the fact that he was bunking in an eleven-year-old's personal landfill.

Henry sat on the old recliner. It was comfortable in spite of the rips and tears and scribbles with colored markers on its tan-colored upholstery. He took a sip of water and set his glass on the maple end table, next to the milk-jug lamp Caitlin had showed him how to turn on with a clap of his hands. This place was going to take some getting used to.

Henry leaned back and studied the photos on the fireplace mantel. One picture caught his eye. A baby wrapped in a blue blanket was being held by a couple. Sam, Henry guessed. And his parents.

It was none of his business, but Henry wanted to know more about the Wheelers. Especially Elisabeth. Something about her intrigued him, something beyond the way she looked, and he wanted to figure out what. "You said your parents were gone. Where did they go?"

She picked up a baby doll from the floor. "Heaven."

He should have guessed. No one would leave these children and a farm on their own. Henry struggled for the correct words to say. He had a reputation for being smooth, but smooth wasn't happening. He'd try sincere. "I'm sorry."

"Thanks." She placed the doll in a plastic laundry basket containing old toys. He thought back to the playroom he'd had built for Noelle when she visited. She wasn't even a year old, but she had more toys than all three Wheeler children.

"What happened to your parents?" Henry was prying, but he didn't care.

She brushed broken pieces of crayons off the coffee table and into a shoe box. "My father and stepmother were killed in a car accident on Highway 18."

"My parents were killed, too," he admitted, remembering the pain, the frustration and the confusion that had followed. "In a plane crash."

She glanced up at him with compassion in her eyes. "Death is always difficult. My mom died of cancer when I was little, but it just seems harder when it's…sudden. Unexpected."

Even though he hadn't been close to his parents, it had been a difficult time for Henry. If not for Brett and Laurel and Cynthia and his other friends… Henry owed them so much. Sending them on adventures had been an easy way to pay them back. And he was an excellent matchmaker. "You must have been so young when this happened."

"I had turned twenty-one two weeks before the accident."

Words failed Henry at the responsibility facing her. Then and now. His life paled in comparison. So did he. He avoided responsibility as much as possible; she grabbed onto it with both hands. "You were so young. You're still so young."

"I'm twenty-four, almost twenty-five. And the kids are growing up so fast." Elisabeth kneeled and picked up multicolored Legos from the braided rug covering the hardwood floor. "One of these days I'm going to look up, and they'll be heading off to college."

"Did you go to college?"

"Yes, but I didn't finish." She sounded so nonchalant, but the longing in her eyes told Henry she was far from indifferent. He couldn't imagine giving everything up for someone else, even if they were relatives.

"Why don't you go back?" he asked.

"The kids, the farm, my job. Maybe once Caitlin starts school, I'll think about it." Elisabeth should be complaining, but she wasn't.

"Do."

"You're sweet to think of me," she said.

She was the only one he wanted to think of. That realization should worry him more than it did. But whatever he was feeling wouldn't last. It never had.

"What about you?" she asked. "You've lost your parents and…everything else. Do you have plans for the future?"

Concern filled her voice, and Henry felt like a jerk. His only plans for the future involved his birthday parties and adventures. A trip to New York for Thanksgiving, Maui and Lanai for two weeks in January, skiing in Telluride in February. "A few."

She didn't look convinced. "Once Manny gets back, I won't need your help."

"I know."

"I have a computer. It's old, but you could put together a résumé."

"Thanks."

Henry was ten years older than she was, but he'd never had to face what she faced on a daily basis. He tried to imagine what her life had been like. One minute a college student, the next a parent for three orphans and an orphan herself. Quitting school to take care of her siblings. Running a farm. Working at a restaurant. "Why do you waitress if you have the farm?"

"Farming isn't the easiest way to make a living. You never know how the crops will do or how much they will be worth. That's why we also plant row crops in addition to the cane berries. Don't want to have all my eggs in one basket." She reached under the table for a red Lego. "And Kathy provides benefits."

"Benefits?"

"Medical and dental insurance," Elisabeth explained. "It's hard to find jobs with benefits in a town this size."

So practical, so sensible, so mature. And only twenty-four. Hard to believe. He had insurance, but didn't even know what it covered. Brett had set him up with everything so he knew whatever policy he had was more than sufficient.

She put a lid on the plastic container holding the Legos. "Your job doesn't come with any benefits."

"I assumed since it paid minimum wage, benefits weren't part of the package."

"They aren't." She rose and placed the container in the toy basket. "If workers come back year after year, I try to pay them more, but it's never enough for their hard work. They deserve so much more than I can afford."

And Elisabeth deserved more than working her life away in order to take care of her family and farm. This amazing young woman was so much more than he could have ever imagined when he'd first seen her this morning. Forget about putting her in a French maid outfit. Nothing less than a halo and wings would do. "What about you?"

She picked up something brown and stuffed—a raggedy teddy bear with a missing ear and ink-drawn eyes. "Me?"

"What do you deserve?"

She clutched the bear to her chest. "I've gotten exactly what I deserve."

Henry didn't like the flatness of her tone or the way her eyes darkened. "That doesn't sound good."

"It's been a long day." She set the bear on top of the other toys in the basket. "There. A little less lived-in."

"A lot less lived-in." And he appreciated her effort.

Elisabeth's grin lit up her face. He thought she was gorgeous, but in that moment she was breathtaking. He'd never seen anything more lovely in all his life. His heart skipped a beat. Three, actually. But who was counting?

"Ready for bed?" she asked.

The air whooshed from Henry's lungs. He didn't move. He couldn't move, couldn't think, couldn't breathe. It was a moment like no other, and he wanted to hang on to it for as long as possible. He wasn't sure what was happening. Something told him he sure as hell didn't want to know. He'd been propositioned before, but this had been totally unexpected. Yet welcomed. Very, very welcomed. He raised a brow. "Isn't it a little early for…bed?"

"Morning will be here before you know it. And there's so much I want to do with you…."

Henry grinned in anticipation.

"Tomorrow."

Disappointment shot through him. Elisabeth wasn't propositioning him. She was talking about sleeping. Not…

She glanced back from the staircase. "Are you coming?"

Was he?

Henry had to decide what he wanted here. Yes, he wanted to prove a point to Cynthia, but winning or losing his adventure wasn't the only thing at stake. Somebody could get hurt. Not him. Surely he was impervious to big blue eyes and soft kissable lips and a slow sweet smile that… Oh, yeah, he was impervious to all that. But he could hurt her. Elisabeth.

Or—the idea seized him—he could help her.

Maybe he was meant to help her.

Elisabeth needed so much more than a boyfriend or

a lover or even a husband. And it wasn't only her. Her brother and sisters were in need, too. The Wheeler family didn't need a farmhand; they needed a fairy godfather.

And Henry knew the perfect man for the job.

"He's gotta be dead."

No, he wasn't dead. But death didn't sound so bad to Henry. He'd only closed his eyes a few minutes ago, and now *they* wanted him to get out of bed. Not even fairy godfathers got up this early.

"If he isn't dead," the high voice he guessed belonged to Caitlin said, "why isn't he moving?"

Because I'm trying to sleep.

Henry didn't want to move; he didn't want to open his eyes. He wanted only for them to go away. Far, far away.

"No one can stay still that long."

Curiosity got the better of him. He blinked open his heavy eyelids and was assaulted by bright, white light.

He squinted, but that did no good. A jagged pain shot through his head, ricocheting off every nerve ending, brain cell and whatever else was inside there. He squeezed his eyes shut. Not even his worst hangover had felt this bad. That's what he got for sleeping without a feather pillow. And these sheets were not Egyptian cotton. A poly-cotton blend, no doubt.

"You're finally awake." The soothing tone of a feminine voice seeped into his foggy brain and made him feel better. He'd fallen asleep thinking about her voice. Her. Elisabeth.

He forced his eyes open. Four pairs of much too clear, much too bright blue eyes stared at him. Henry glanced around for a clock, but only saw a candy bar wrapper, a pile of comic books and stacks of cards—baseball and monster creatures. "What time is it?"

"Seven," Elisabeth said.

In the morning? Henry couldn't remember the last time he'd woken up before nine o'clock. He slept late unless he had a plane to catch or an event to attend. And he always tried to schedule those at decent hours. He cleared his dry, scratchy throat and wished he could do the same with his tired, foggy brain. "Is this what time you normally get up?"

"Usually it's earlier," Abby said.

Any earlier and they may as well not even go to bed. Henry never fell asleep until after one o'clock in the morning. "Even on weekends?"

"On Saturdays, we sometimes sleep in until seven-thirty or eight," Elisabeth said. "It depends what we need to get done."

Sam rolled his eyes. "She means chores."

Okay, Henry just realized a big downside to farming. He'd have to adjust his hours.

"Would you like to go to church with us?" Elisabeth asked.

Henry thought for a moment. "Is someone getting married?"

"No," she said.

He sat up and hit his head on the upper bunk. Rubbing his throbbing forehead, he lay down. "Did someone die?"

"No," Abby said.

"Baptism?"

Another no. This time from Sam.

"Then why are you going to church?" he asked.

"It's Sunday," Caitlin answered.

Sunday meant sleeping even later than he normally did. It meant eating brunch and sipping mimosas. What he wouldn't give for a cappuccino right now. Forget that, he wanted more sleep.

"There's a breakfast afterwards," Abby said. "Mayor Logan makes her famous buttermilk pancakes."

Henry adjusted the covers. "Thanks, but I'll pass."

"No problem," Elisabeth said. "I'll leave a list of things for you to do while we're gone."

"Fine." Tops on his to-do list was going back to sleep.

"See you later," she said.

"Later." He buried his head against the pillow, closed his eyes and half waved. Much later.

Chapter Five

Eleven o'clock, and Elisabeth was exhausted. She ushered the kids out of the Suburban. Word of her new hired hand had spread faster than mold growing on berries. As soon as she'd entered the church, the barrage of questions had made her want to turn and run home.

She didn't know enough about Henry Davenport to provide adequate answers and that had only added to her friends' and neighbors' concerns. It was difficult when everyone in Berry Patch considered themselves to be extended family.

But she couldn't worry about them. Elisabeth had her hands full with her own family. They had to be her only concern. Not small town curiosity. Not her gawking, lovesick behavior this morning in Sam's bedroom.

Heaven help her.

Seeing the shadow of Henry's lashes on his cheeks and the rise and fall of his bare chest had made Elisabeth feel all fluttery inside. But fluttery wouldn't cut it. Not one bit.

Caitlin tugged on her hand. "Let's play in the creek!"

"What creek?" Elisabeth asked.

Caitlin pointed to a stream of water rushing from her vegetable garden. "That one."

"Oh, no." Elisabeth ran squishing her way through the mud and pooling water in her only pair of dress shoes. Forget about the shoes. They were a dirty mess, but that was the least of her problems. She would have to replant. They lived off the food they grew. Even during the rainy autumn and winter seasons. She shut off the spigot.

How could this have happened? Turning off the water was the first thing on her to-do list for Henry.

"Is it bad?" Sam asked.

Yes, it was bad, but the kids didn't need to know the truth. Life was hard enough for them. She struggled against the frustration seizing control of her. She couldn't lose it. Not in front of her brother and sisters. Elisabeth shrugged. "We'll have to replant a few things."

"I like to plant seeds." Caitlin bent over near the edge of the flooded garden.

Elisabeth reached for her sister. "Be careful—"

Plop. Caitlin fell knees-first and sank into the mud. "Owwww." Crocodile tears streamed down her cheeks. "My knee. My pretty dress. And tights. Th-they're ruined."

Elisabeth picked her up. "We can wash the tights and the dress."

"I'm b-bleeding." Caitlin sniffled. "I need a Band-Aid."

Band-Aids usually made any boo-boo feel better whether they were needed or not. "When we get inside…"

"The house is on fire." Panic filled Abby's voice.

"Fire," Sam screamed only to be drowned out by the screeching smoke detector.

Smoke, thick and black, billowed out the kitchen window. Elisabeth set Caitlin on her feet away from the mud. "Grab the hose, Sam. Keep Caitlin away, Abby."

As Elisabeth ran to the house, her heart pounded in her chest. Everything they owned, every photograph of their parents was in the house. But so was a living, breathing person.

"Henry!" She yelled the name again. And again.

The back door flew open. Smoke, not as much as before, filtered out. The smoke detector fell silent.

Henry stood in the doorway with a burned towel in his hand. "Did you have a nice time at church?"

Who could think of church at a time like this? Elisabeth's pulse and heart rate had yet to slow down. Henry, however, seemed unaffected by any of this. That bothered her. A lot. Not to mention the fact that he was wearing her apron, and it was covered with... She wasn't sure what it was. "What's going on?"

Her voice was steady, calm, not high-pitched. The house had been on fire, and she hadn't lost it. A definite improvement considering her reaction to Sam's failing grade on last week's math test.

"I wanted eggs Benedict for breakfast," Henry said.

Caitlin frowned. "Sounds yucky."

Abby got a thoughtful expression on her face. "They say Benedict Arnold was a traitor, but there's compelling evidence to suggest—"

"Quiet," Elisabeth ordered. "What happened?"

"I was making myself breakfast," Henry explained. "I love eggs Benedict, but I didn't know how to make a hollandaise sauce so I figured an omelet and toast would be a good substitute. But I realized I didn't know how to make an omelet. Or toast. I'm not much of a cook. In fact, I've never cooked in my life."

His knock-your-socks-off smile sent her pulse rate climbing again.

Elisabeth didn't like that. Or him. He was so much like Toby, a boy who would never grow up. "First you flood my garden and then you try to burn down my house by cooking when you don't know how to cook. What's next? Do you have a swarm of locusts packed away in your bag that you're going to let loose on the crops?"

He furrowed his brow. "What flood?"

"I'd asked you to turn off the water when you got up. It was on the list I left for you on the kitchen table."

"I was going to read the list after I ate breakfast." He stared at the singed towel. "I just got up."

"It's after eleven," she said.

"I generally sleep in on weekends."

Now she was going to lose it. She could feel her temper bubbling up. She bit the inside of her cheek and counted backwards from ten. It didn't help.

Sam burst into the kitchen with a garden hose in his hands. Water dripped from the hand trigger. "Where's the fire?"

"I wouldn't call it a real fire," Henry said. "The flames only licked the ceiling."

"What's with the apron?" Sam asked.

"He was cooking breakfast," Caitlin answered.

"Doesn't Henry look like Daddy did when he wore Mommy's apron to make us cinnamon rolls?" Abby asked.

A rare smile lit up Sam's face. "Dad burned them."

Caitlin giggled. "Just like Henry."

Abby laughed. "The fire alarm went off. Smoke was everywhere. It smelled bad. Mommy was so mad."

Caitlin giggled again. "Just like Elisabeth."

The smiles disappeared. The laughter, too. Mommy and Daddy weren't ever coming home again. And it was Elisabeth's fault. A heaviness settled on her heart.

"I'd better put the hose away," Sam muttered.

Abby held Caitlin's hand. "We'll go with you."

Elisabeth stared out the window at the slumped shoulders of the three people she loved most in this world. No matter how hard she tried she could never take the place of their parents.

"I'm sorry," Henry said.

Me, too.

Words weren't enough. They didn't have enough money to afford fresh fruit and vegetables at the grocery store. That's why they grew their own. "You will have to replant the garden. We count on that food."

"Of course," he said.

As she turned, her gaze caught his. Staring into his eyes made her feel warm and tingly. What was she doing? What was she feeling? Henry was way more trouble than he was worth. She didn't need any more problems than the ones she already had.

"Is there anything you want me to do?" he asked.

"I left you a list."

"I'm going to get to it." He flashed a killer smile. "But I thought there might be something you wanted me to do first."

"There is." Elisabeth refused to be charmed. She squared her shoulders. "Clean up this mess."

* * *

Cleaning up his mess wasn't so easy to do. Especially when Henry had to use rags—dirty, disgusting rags. He tried to find a clean spot on the one in his hands. Tried and failed.

"Do you have any paper towels?" he asked.

Elisabeth stopped putting sliced vegetables into a Crock-Pot and tossed him another rag. "These are more cost effective."

That might be true, but they were also gross. He could buy a lot of paper towels with his twenty-dollar bill.

Maybe paper towels would bring a smile to Elisabeth's face. She was upset with him. He might not know farming, but he knew women. The way she kept glancing over at him and pressing her full lips together were telltale signs. No problem. He'd gotten off to a rocky start, but he'd learned his lesson—no more cooking. Before the day was over, she would have a different opinion of him.

Henry scrubbed the stove top. The burn marks wouldn't come off. At this rate he would be here all day. Of course that didn't surprise him. The only thing he knew how to clean was himself.

Until this morning, Henry hadn't realized how much he relied on his household staff. He was totally dependent upon them and had taken them for granted his entire life. He didn't have to cook or clean or even pay his bills. Someone else did that for him. Someone else did everything for him. Whatever Henry wanted—from fresh towels to late night snacks—was there when he wanted it. If he were at home freshly ground coffee would be brewing, a three-course breakfast would be waiting for him at the dining room table and Mrs. Zimmer would be making his bed and tidying up his room.

His life was so easy and carefree. Fun. Life on the farm seemed precarious and worrisome. A way to grow old before one's time. Not fun.

Elisabeth grabbed a bottle from underneath the sink. She squeezed the trigger twice. "Now wipe."

He did, and the marks disappeared. Henry couldn't believe it. All that scrubbing for nothing. "This stuff is amazing."

"It's vinegar and water." She handed him the bottle. "You're not used to doing this, are you?"

Never had before. "No."

The expression in her eyes softened. "I'm so sorry, Henry. I forgot you don't have a home to clean."

"That's...okay." Henry felt anything but. He wasn't exactly lying to her. He didn't have a home to clean right now. Semantics? He looked at the stove, at the sink, at everything except Elisabeth. "I've never been much of a housekeeper."

"I'll help you finish," Elisabeth said. "We have a lot to do today."

Not only today. Henry had a month to make the Wheeler family's life better. That wasn't going to be an easy task.

He stood on a step stool and wiped the spot where the flames had licked the ceiling. The cleaner took the marks right off.

She handed him another rag. "Here you go."

"Thanks." His gaze met hers. She was lovely. If only she would smile more, but smiles and laughter were rare commodities around here. At least Caitlin seemed less affected than the others. "Did I miss any spots?" he asked.

Elisabeth looked up at the ceiling. "To the left."

"I see it." Another spray of the vinegar and water combo, and he wiped the spot away. "Got it."

She rinsed her hands in the sink. "Now we can really get to work."

Henry couldn't wait. Domestic chores weren't his strong suit. He followed her outside. "It might be better if my job assignments didn't involve the kitchen."

Elisabeth's eyes twinkled. "I was thinking the same thing."

She showed him the irrigation equipment and together they moved it to a different part of the farm. It was more physical work than anything and took longer than he thought it would and his hands sort of burned, but completing the task gave Henry a needed burst of confidence. He wasn't used to manual labor, but he was strong. If she needed muscle to help her out, he was her man. Fairy godfather, he corrected himself.

Next up was mowing. Standing by the small tractor, Elisabeth explained what the various levers did and how the two brake pedals could be unlatched for use in the fields.

As she bent over to double check the hitch connecting the mower to the tractor, sunlight glimmered off her hair. Once again her beauty struck him. Not to mention the curve of her hips beneath her well-worn jeans.

But he wasn't here to admire her or be attracted to her. He was here to do a job. Two jobs, actually. Farmhand and fairy godfather. Good thing the two could be done concurrently or he'd have his work cut out for him.

Elisabeth stood. "Any questions?"

A gentle breeze carried the scent of her toward him. He didn't recognize the subtle fragrance, but it suited her. Light, simple, a hint of vanilla. Different from the expensive designer perfumes the women he dated wore, but he liked it. A lot. "You smell good."

Henry realized he should have been paying attention to her instructions, not her scent.

"It's lotion." She looked away, but not before a charming pink tinged her cheeks. "The kids gave it to me."

The idea of Elisabeth rubbing lotion over her skin sent Henry's temperature up a degree—several, actually.

Stop. Now. He was supposed to be helping her, not lusting after her. He should pay attention to her, not imagine her rubbing lotion on her skin.

Besides he wasn't here only to help the Wheelers; he was here to win Cynthia's adventure. Losing wasn't an option. No matter what it took, he would win. And at the same time become an indispensable asset to Elisabeth's berry farm.

"The kids have good taste." Henry picked up the keys to the tractor. "I'm ready to mow."

The corners of her mouth lifted. "Think you can handle it?"

All he had to do was pull the mower between the rows of berries. A monkey could manage that. Henry smiled. "Yes."

"Let me know if you need anything."

A kiss for good luck? No, he didn't need luck to accomplish this task. He wouldn't need anything except a cool beverage once he was finished. A nice bottle of Cristal would be nice. But he would have to wait an entire month for that. Even if he spent his twenty on champagne he couldn't afford a bottle of his favorite bubbly.

Henry climbed onto the tractor and turned the key in the ignition. The engine roared. The machine vibrated. It was way too loud. He loved it.

He hit the gas, but the machine didn't move. The mower. He gave it more gas and the tractor moved forward. He tested the brakes. Instead of stopping, he turned in a circle. Damn. The brakes were unhitched. "Just checking the turning radius."

She nodded, but he saw the doubt in her eyes. "Be careful."

"I will."

She started to speak, but stopped herself.

No problem. Henry would show Elisabeth how well he could handle all of this. The fun was just beginning. Not only for him, but the entire Wheeler family. Their fairy godfather was on the job and about to work miracles.

"It's a miracle you found Henry." Theresa Logan, Elisabeth's best friend since kindergarten, leaned against her brother Gabriel's pickup truck parked outside the barn while Abby and Caitlin played on the hay bales they were unloading. "Sounds like he is the answer to your prayers."

Elisabeth pushed a bale of hay to the edge of the tailgate. "I wouldn't go that far."

"Neither would I." Gabriel Logan lifted the bale as if it were a bag of feed. Sam was right next to him, as usual. "I still don't understand why you hired this Henry guy. You had lots of people offer to help you. Me, Dad, the entire town."

Elisabeth hopped down from the truck bed. "People have their own farms and businesses to take care of. I don't want to be a burden."

"You're not a burden." Gabriel brushed the hay from his navy T-shirt. "Friends help each other. That's how it works. Unless one friend happens to be too stubborn for her own good."

Though she loved Gabriel like a brother, she'd heard this speech before. Too many times. "Henry will only be here until Manny's back."

"You don't know when Manny will be back," Gabriel said. "Henry is a total stranger."

"I checked his references."

"He knows nothing about farming."

But thanks to Cynthia Sterling it wasn't costing Elisabeth anything to have him here. Except her food stores, the paint on her kitchen ceiling, her favorite pan. She pushed another hay bale out. "He's doing fine. Henry was a big help with the irrigation equipment."

"I heard he let the chickens out," Gabriel said.

She ignored the niggling doubt that had been creeping up all afternoon. "I didn't warn him about the gate."

Gabriel stuck his thumb through the belt loop of his jeans. "What about breaking the spray nozzle?"

"Henry offered to pay for the damage with his next paycheck." But as she said the words, she knew money couldn't buy back the time they'd lost today. She was more behind than ever. Elisabeth glanced at Sam. "What have you been telling Gabriel?"

Sam stuck out his chin. "The truth."

That's all she needed. Gabriel's doubts to add to her own. Still she felt the need to defend Henry. He might not know what he was doing, but he was trying hard. That had to count for something. "It's Henry's first day on the job. Everyone needs time to adjust."

Gabriel stared at her. "That sounds like an excuse."

It was. She feared Henry would never adjust. He didn't seem cut out for farming. He didn't seem cut out for farming, cooking, cleaning, anything and everything. Trouble followed him—indoors, outdoors, everywhere.

"Henry will figure things out." She said that more for her benefit than anyone else's. Ten thousand dollars bought a lot of extra chances. Maybe she should ask Abby to run a cost-benefit analysis to see where the money and Henry's mistakes met.

Theresa glanced through a pair of binoculars the girls had found in the cab of Gabriel's truck. "I know why you hired Henry."

"Why's that?" Gabriel asked.

Theresa grinned. "He's gorgeous."

"I want to see," Caitlin said, bouncing up and down. Theresa handed her the binoculars.

"That's not why I hired him," Elisabeth said.

"Sure." Theresa winked. "I'm so happy to see a good-looking single man. The pickings are slim in Berry Patch."

"There's more than enough single women," Gabriel said. Theresa rolled her eyes. "I'm sure Henry will be giving you serious competition for the most eligible bachelor title, big brother."

"I doubt that." Gabriel glanced toward the field. "He's homeless and penniless."

"But with that face and body." Theresa sighed.

Uh-oh. Warning bells sounded in Elisabeth's head. Theresa was a die-hard romantic who dreamed of finding her Prince Charming and one for Elisabeth, too. That's because Theresa fancied herself a modern-day version of Jane Austen's Emma. But what if Theresa wanted Henry for herself?

Caitlin giggled, staring through the binoculars at the berries. "Henry's so funny."

Elisabeth glanced over to the crops. Henry, sans tractor, was running, his arms flailing and swatting at the air as a dark cloud followed him.

Oh, no. "Bees," she said.

"At least he can run fast," Gabriel said.

"That's about all Henry can do," Sam said. "Except snore."

Gabriel laughed.

"This isn't funny," Elisabeth said. "What if he's allergic to bees? We have to help him."

"Not much we can do except upset the bees more," Gabriel said.

"He'll outrun them," Abby said confidently.

"What if he gets stung?" Caitlin asked.

Henry slapped his arm and stumbled, but managed to keep moving forward.

Gabriel grimaced. "I think he just did."

"Cool," Sam said.

It wasn't cool. Not at all. Elisabeth felt so useless watching Henry try to outrun the bees. But Gabriel was right. There was nothing they could do.

"Running from bees or not—" Theresa pinched her cheeks to give them color "—Henry looks attractive."

"He looks like an idiot," Gabriel said.

"No, he doesn't," Elisabeth said even though most other men did look like idiots compared to Gabriel Logan. He was ruggedly handsome with beautiful blue eyes and a grin that made women, with the exception of Elisabeth and his five sisters, swoon.

"I agree. Not an idiot." Theresa combed her fingers through her short brown hair. "It's more of a run-for-your-life-I-think-I'm-going-to-die kind of cuteness."

Abby took a step forward. "The bees are slowing down."

"They must be tired of chasing him."

But Henry continued running after the bees had

stopped. A part of Elisabeth wished he would run right off the edge of her property and keep going.

"I can't believe he hasn't slowed down," Theresa said. "He must be in really good shape."

Henry raced toward the barn. Sweat dampened his hair, beaded on his face, drenched his shirt. Dirt covered the thighs of his jeans. His cheeks were red. His breathing haggard. He skidded to a stop. He braced himself with his hands on his knees and leaned over to catch his breath.

"Are you okay?" Elisabeth asked.

He nodded. "Talk about a workout. They should add a swarm of bees to the Olympics. Bet we'd see a new world record."

She glanced at his face and arms, but couldn't see any red marks. "Did you get stung?"

Henry stuck out his hand. Two spots were red and swollen. "They'll be okay."

She moved closer and took his injured hand in hers. He smelled of sweat, dirt and fresh grass. The scent was more appealing than it should have been. She let go of his hand. "What happened?"

"I cut a corner too close." Henry straightened. "The mower knocked over a stack of hives. I didn't see any bees flying around so I thought I'd put them back."

"You never touch a hive," Abby said.

"Never ever," Caitlin added.

"I know that now."

Today had been nothing but one lesson after another for Henry. Talk about a learning curve. Elisabeth hoped he improved tomorrow. She handed him a spare bottle of water. "Is the tractor okay?"

He nodded and drank half the bottle. "The hives don't

look damaged either, but I couldn't see all of them. They are still on the ground."

"Just leave them." Elisabeth didn't want him near the bees. Near anything. Maybe it was time for that cost-benefit analysis. "I'll call the beekeeper."

As Henry glanced around, his eyes widened and the red on his cheeks deepened. "I didn't realize you had company." He managed a smile and Elisabeth respected that after having made a fool of himself in front of everybody with the bees. "I'm Henry."

"Theresa Logan. Best friend and sometimes baby-sitter." She wet her lips. "This is my brother."

"Gabe Logan." His tone was wary, but he extended his arm.

Henry wiped his hand on his jeans and shook Gabriel's hand. Henry winced at the contact. No doubt the bee stings did hurt. Still he kept smiling. "Nice to meet you."

The two men were a stark contrast. Even dirty and sweating and wearing jeans, Henry would be more comfortable in the city. Anywhere but on a berry farm. Gabriel was outdoors and country-living-personified whether in jeans or... Elisabeth realized she had never seen him in anything dressy except on his ill-fated wedding day. After his divorce, Gabe swore never to wear a tuxedo again. But no matter what either wore, or didn't wear, both men would be popular with the women of Berry Patch. With women everywhere.

Theresa batted her eyes. "So what brings you to Berry Patch? The bees?"

"The bees were a first, and I hope, a last." Henry stared at Theresa as if she were the only woman on the planet. "I'm here because a friend heard Elisabeth needed help and I needed a job."

Yes, he was here to help her. Not flirt with her best friend.

"Sounds like fate." Theresa's voice sounded wistful.

Gabriel frowned. "More like dumb luck."

"Probably a combination of both," Henry said. "Are you a farmer?"

"Contractor," Gabriel said. "I have a remodeling business, but I help my father with his hops farm."

"Gabe fixed Old Yeller, too, " Sam said.

Lines creased Henry's forehead. "Are you also a vet?"

The kids giggled. Gabriel and Theresa managed not to laugh.

Elisabeth frowned. Poor Henry. He wasn't having the best day. "Old Yeller is a pickup truck that's on its last legs."

"Rather wheels," Theresa added with a flip of her hair.

Henry laughed. "Let me guess, the truck is old and yellow."

"Henry graduated from Harvard," Abby announced.

Elisabeth cringed. Henry had to be humiliated. She caught a glimpse of sadness in his eyes, but the moment their gazes met, it disappeared. She gave him an encouraging smile and Henry laughed. Laughed?

"Too bad I concentrated in romance languages and literature. Harvard doesn't teach you how to drive a tractor or outrun bees." Henry was so animated, his voice upbeat, his smile dazzling. "You think I could get a refund?"

Everyone laughed.

"I'm sure you could get whatever you wanted," Theresa said, almost breathlessly. Subtlety was not one of her strong points.

"You think?" Henry asked Theresa.

Uncomfortable, Elisabeth ground the toe of her work boot into the dirt. Gabriel rocked back and raised a brow.

"Pretty smooth," he murmured to her.

Too smooth. Henry wasn't only a screwup. He was also a flirt. A charmer. A player. The job didn't matter to him. The farm didn't matter to him. She didn't matter to him.

He had to go.

But she needed the money. And then she remembered. *If Henry quits, you can keep the check.*

Chapter Six

"Dog-doo, horse-doo, cat-doo. I've had it with doo-doo." Henry propped the shovel against the barn, stripped off his filthy gloves and threw them on the ground. "Being a fairy godfather has never been this hard before."

Henry's new best friend stared up at him with sleepy brown eyes.

"You look how I feel." He rubbed the mangy mutt's head. His third day on the farm, Henry had noticed a lump of fur in a corner of the barn. He'd thought it was a dead animal, but the dog, Ruffian, had only been sleeping. "Too bad there's no time to be tired. Only time to work."

Work.

Henry hated working. He hated everything about life on the farm. The never-ending exhaustion, the won't-wash-off dirt, the thin, sandpaper-like towels hanging in the bathroom.

It didn't help that he was the worst farmhand in the history of agriculture. So far he'd done nothing but cause trouble and make mistakes. Mistakes in front of the family, their friends and Elisabeth. She'd seen him get chased and stung by bees, pop a wheelie when he dropped the rototiller and nearly crushed Ruff, upset the chickens in the henhouse, break a day's worth of eggs and fall face first while mucking out the barn.

Henry turned on the faucet outside the barn and rinsed his hands.

This job was hell on his ego. Who was he kidding? He hadn't an ounce of pride left.

But Henry was all Elisabeth had. He couldn't let her down. Or Sam. Or Abby. Or Caitlin. Or Ruff. Or that damn nameless gray cat that slept on his chest every night.

Quitting had never sounded so good to him. But it wasn't an option. Forget about faking an injury and spending a much-needed day in bed. He couldn't think about writing a check and making it all better because of the stupid adventure, either.

"It sucks, but I'm stuck." Henry dried his hands on a dingy monogrammed linen handkerchief that had once been white. "At least until Manny returns."

Damn Cynthia.

Henry didn't need this. He didn't want to see how the other half lived. He didn't want to know how the other half struggled. He didn't want to be the other half.

If she was trying to teach him a lesson, he'd learned one. He was happy he was rich and didn't have to deal with life the way Elisabeth had to. He was only supposed to be here for a month, but she faced this day in and day out. Henry didn't know how she did it or why she wanted to keep doing it.

He couldn't wait to get back to his real life. Because he could do more for Elisabeth and her family as Henry the billionaire than he ever could as Henry the farm-hand. "I could stay here forever and never be good enough for this job."

Ruff groaned.

"Don't worry, boy. I may not be cut out for farming, but she put her trust in me to do this job and that's what I'll do." Henry removed his hands from the water. Dirt was still ground under his fingernails and embedded in the dry cracks of his hands, but that was as good as it would get. "Even if it kills me."

Which, Henry realized grimly, it just might.

Ruff's ears perked up. Footsteps sounded on the gravel and Henry looked that way. Elisabeth walked toward him. She wore jeans and a red field jacket. Her hair was pulled back into a braid and once again she wore no makeup. She looked more beautiful than any woman had the right to look. He only wished she didn't have those dark circles under her eyes. Henry shoved the handkerchief into his back pocket.

She greeted him with a smile. "Good morning, Henry."

Seeing her made the morning better. Now if he could get his act together and do something right, things would be a little more tolerable. "Morning."

"How are you today?" she asked.

Bone-weary and hating life. His best effort wasn't good enough. For the farm or Elisabeth. Just as his parents had always said. Henry forced a smile. "Just fine."

"You missed breakfast."

He'd fallen back asleep after the alarm went off. It had been physically impossible for him to crawl out of bed. Especially with Ruff dozing on his legs and the fat gray nameless cat asleep on his chest. But when he finally woke up he skipped breakfast so he wouldn't start the morning behind schedule. "I wasn't hungry."

His stomach growled.

She removed something wrapped in a paper towel from her jacket pocket and handed it to him. "In case you get hungry."

Elisabeth was so sweet, always thinking of others. He unwrapped the paper towel and saw a rectangular piece of something. The white icing with red sparkles looked interesting. But edible? He was almost too hungry to care whether it was or not. "What is it?"

She drew her eyebrows together. "A Pop Tart."

He'd heard of them, but never tasted one. Henry took a bite. Not bad. "It's good. Thanks."

As he ate, Ruff nudged his leg, and Henry tossed him a bite to eat.

"I can't believe the difference in that dog," Elisabeth admitted. "Ruff used to stay around the barn. He would only come inside the house to eat. Even during winter."

"He likes sleeping in the house now," Henry said.

"He likes sleeping with you."

And so would you. Henry petted Ruff. "It's nice to have a warm body next to you."

"He's a smart dog." She smiled. "My dad found him when he was a puppy. Ruff followed him like a shadow. He loved my dad and tolerated the rest of us. Until you."

"Poor boy must have been lonely."

Elisabeth nodded and adjusted her gloves. "Are you ready to get to work?"

"I've been working since six o'clock," he said.

"I meant working in the fields."

Just the mention of the word *fields* made his muscles tighten in protest. He would never look at a berry or any produce the same way.

"We're going to tie today," she said.

Henry didn't want to tie the canes. He wanted to kick the canes. There had to be an easier way. Like buying the farm from Elisabeth for an inflated price and burning it to the ground.

Stop. He couldn't think that way. The Wheelers needed help, and he was all they had. He had to get through this.

Henry put on a pair of new work gloves, hopped on an ATV and followed Elisabeth on her four-wheeler to the loganberries. *Try and look at the bright side.* He got to have fun riding from the barn and back. That was something good. Too bad everything in between sucked. He sighed.

Mist had settled between the rows of canes. Henry glanced up. The sky was gray. Rain? He hoped not, but knowing his luck…

"It's not hard once you get the hang of it. I'll show you." With a paper tie in one hand, she reached around the berry bush with the other and secured the vine to the wire trellis without a wasted motion. "The canes grow so fast that if we get behind and they get too big, it takes two people to tie each cane."

"So we have to get it done before that happens."

"Exactly." She handed him a paper tie. "Your turn."

Henry took a tie, grabbed a cane and threw the additional growth over the trellis wire. A cluster of thorny vines racked his face, scratching his left cheek. "Damn."

"Are you okay?" Elisabeth asked.

It hurt like hell. "I'm okay."

"You threw the vine the wrong way."

He did everything the wrong way. But not his birthday parties and adventures. Without those in his life…no, this wasn't only about Cynthia's adventure any more.

Elisabeth's eyes darkened. "Your cheek is bleeding."

"I'll survive."

Somehow he would find a way to survive it all. The farm. The work. Her.

"You should head back to the house and clean that scratch."

"At lunchtime."

"Suit yourself."

He wished he could suit himself. In one of his Armani suits to be exact. Better yet a tuxedo. He had seven to choose from. Anything to show Elisabeth the man he really was so she would see him as a desirable man instead of a fumbling idiot.

He was charming, sexy Henry. Women wanted him. Or at least pretended it wasn't his Davenport name and fortune they were really after. But not Elisabeth with an *S*.

Even with his money, he wasn't the man Elisabeth needed. But he was all she had. He would not let her down. He would prove to himself he was more than a fat wallet and a bloated trust fund. Henry focused on the next cane to be tied.

Elisabeth touched his shoulder. "Are you sure you're okay?"

Concern filled her voice. Henry felt a little hitch in his heart. "I'll be fine. I just need to figure out the correct way to tie."

The corners of her mouth lifted. "I'll help you figure it out."

She stood behind him and placed her arms alongside

his. Even with their jackets and clothing between them, he could feel the softness of her breasts pressing against his back. Her sweet scent surrounded him. If only they could work like this all day…

"Take the vine with this hand and toss it over the trellis like this." With her hand on his arm, she led him through the motion. "Now tie it onto the wire."

Henry was having trouble breathing, let alone accomplishing any sort of task requiring brain cells. The blood had rushed from his head to the one place he didn't want it to go. He wasn't sure how he managed to tie the vine, but he did.

As Elisabeth stepped back, emotion surged through Henry. An odd mixture of relief and regret. Holding her felt good, but so did helping her. If only he could do both…

"The bleeding stopped." Elisabeth removed her glove and touched his face. "I don't think it will scar."

She stood so close to him and smelled so good, it was worth a scar. Henry grinned. "A scar wouldn't be bad. Women find scars sexy."

"Some women do, but not all." She tilted her chin, put on her glove and got to work.

"Which do you prefer? Scar or no scar?"

"It depends."

"On what?" he asked.

"The man."

It wasn't the answer he wanted. Henry wanted her to like him. Hell, he wanted her to want him. What was he going to do?

What was she going to do? That evening Elisabeth shoved the marionberry pie into the oven and slammed the door closed.

Henry should have been long gone. But he hadn't left. He hadn't slunk away in the middle of the night. He hadn't quit. Elisabeth twisted the knob on the timer and overshot the time by fifteen minutes. She reset it to the correct time.

He was supposed to quit, not dive into whatever task she gave him. Okay, he wasn't diving. He was drowning. Still he hadn't given up. Not even after she'd thrown in chores that hadn't been done in years.

Darn him.

She scrubbed the flour off the countertop. Too bad she couldn't get rid of Henry as easily.

Why hadn't he quit?

That was the only way she could keep Cynthia Sterling's check and use it to hire someone who knew what he was doing. If there was any money left over, she could fix the roof and the plumbing and a million other things.

But that wasn't going to happen. Not now. Elisabeth's shoulders slumped.

There was nothing left for her to do to discourage him. To try and make him quit. And that left one course of action—to fire him. She couldn't keep him around any longer.

Thinking about firing him made her feel awful. Elisabeth sagged against the counter. Not that she wasn't justified in letting Henry go. He had made mistake after mistake. She still couldn't believe he'd cut back the wrong row of berries. Farming clearly wasn't his thing. But even though he hadn't a clue about what he was doing, he was trying hard. That had to count for something. She sighed. Ten thousand dollars worth of something?

She might be down on her luck, but so was Henry.

Maybe she could convince him to accept Cynthia's help—even take the money from the check. No, he didn't want charity. That's why Elisabeth couldn't ask him to quit. She didn't want him to know what his friends had done for him.

As she removed the lid from the pot on the stove, the scent of the Mexican stew filled the air. Cinnamon, oregano, cumin, jalapeño chilis. She stirred the simmering broth, added diced chicken and replaced the lid.

The whine of a lone four-wheeler caught her attention. She glanced at the clock. Henry had worked later than she expected.

Perhaps she had misjudged him. Okay, he had flirted with her best friend, but he hadn't destroyed the farm. At least not yet. Maybe he wouldn't. Maybe he would learn. Maybe he could stay.

Her chest tightened. That reaction alone told her it was time for Henry to pack his bag and go. She couldn't afford to have feelings for a charmer like him. Not that she had feelings. But it could happen. And that would be a huge mistake. Henry might be here now, but she couldn't count on him to be here in the long run. Of that, she had no doubt.

The kitchen door opened, and Henry stepped inside with Ruff panting at his heels. He had removed his work boots and wore white socks on his feet. Dirt covered his jeans and jacket. A jacket sleeve had been ripped. His face had smudges on it. His hair was damp on the ends. He smelled like he looked—as if he'd been working hard since dawn. Attraction hit hard. Elisabeth swallowed around the blackberry-sized lump in her throat.

"Did you see the sunset?" He stared at her. "Beautiful."

He was beautiful. Gorgeous. You name it. Simply the

richness of his voice made her pulse speed up. Another reason to fire him. "I—I didn't notice."

"I finished tying the rows you wanted."

"All of them?"

He nodded.

"That's good." Incredible, actually. She thought it would take him longer. A lot longer.

And then it hit her. Henry had done a good job. He hadn't screwed up. He had been helpful today. Yet the last thing she felt was relief. Not when her insides were reacting to his every word, glance, movement.

Ruff nuzzled his nose against Henry. As he petted the dog, Henry grimaced.

Elisabeth took a step toward him and stopped. "Is something wrong with your hand?"

"A blister," he said. "It's nothing."

"You're not used to this kind of work. I'd better check it." She reached for his hand. A jolt of electricity shocked her at the point of contact, and she ignored it. He had two small blisters on his left hand, three larger ones on his right. "Why didn't you stop working? This had to hurt."

"The canes needed to be tied." His gaze met hers. "We can't afford to get behind. Isn't that what you said?"

She nodded.

"I know I've messed up, but I'm getting it. I won't screw up again." He paused. "At least not intentionally."

Yes, his hands were a mess, but that hadn't mattered to him. He'd put the farm first. And her.

She couldn't fire him.

Henry was staying. For now. Frustration sped down her spine followed by a surge of relief. It had to be about the check. There couldn't be another reason for the jumble of emotions she felt. There just couldn't be.

"Let's get your blisters fixed up."

In the kitchen, Elisabeth cleaned the blisters with antibacterial soap. "Does this hurt?"

"No."

She wondered if he would tell her if it did hurt. As she rinsed his hands with water, she noticed how large they were. He might not be used to manual labor but his hands looked strong. And felt warm. She turned off the water. "Better."

He nodded.

"You have nice hands."

"So do you."

What was she doing? Saying? They were just hands. Male hands. They were supposed to be big and strong and warm. She patted his hands dry, placed a dab of ointment on them and covered them with bandages. Elisabeth put everything back in the first-aid kit. "That should help them heal faster."

He flexed his fingers. "Thanks."

"You need to be more careful," she said, focusing on his blisters. "If you feel any burning or aching, stop what you are doing and see if a blister is forming. Plus you don't want these to get infected."

"I'll try to remember that." His gaze captured hers. "I don't always think things through like I should."

"That can get you into trouble."

"Sometimes it gets me what I want." He smiled. "Like now."

Before she could say anything, Henry lowered his lips to hers.

Step back, a voice in her head warned. But Elisabeth didn't. One little kiss wouldn't hurt anything. Wouldn't hurt her.

Soft. His lips were soft against hers. And warm.

Henry didn't push. He didn't do anything except send tingles running all over her body. He cupped the back of her head and wove his fingers through her hair. She soaked up the feel and the taste of him. It had been so long since she'd been kissed.

Too long.

And she wanted more.

Elisabeth parted her lips. She splayed her hands on his back and pulled him toward her. Henry took the hint and increased the pressure. Increased…everything.

He tasted. He teased. He explored.

But most of all he kissed.

Oh, boy, could Henry kiss.

Her knees had never gone weak before. But they were weak now. She'd heard of women swooning. She never thought she'd be one of them. Thank goodness her back was against the counter or she'd be on the floor. Maybe that wouldn't be such a bad thing.

Henry left no part of her mouth untouched. She didn't want to think about how he got to be such a great kisser. But he was so good. Maybe this is what they taught at Harvard. Maybe he had been born that way.

That had to be it. A natural talent for kissing.

She clung to Henry's wide shoulders. She didn't want to let go. She didn't want this kiss to end. Not ever.

One little kiss wasn't so little.

Henry's kiss washed away her loneliness. She felt a sense of security that had been missing for way too long. She was no longer a big sister, a farmer, a wait-ress, a stand-in mom. She was simply Elisabeth. A woman. And she liked the feeling. Liked it a lot.

He pulled her closer and she went willingly. The

years of wishing things could be different, but knowing they couldn't faded. In this one moment, her life could be different. She could be different. She could believe in a happily-ever-after ending. She could believe in happiness again. She could believe in almost anything.

Henry backed away. His eyes were wide, his breathing as ragged as her own. "I'm sorry, Elisabeth."

She was sorry, too. Sorry his kiss had to end. She touched her throbbing, swollen lips wishing Henry's lips were against them, not her fingertip. She glanced up at him. "You're apologizing?"

"I shouldn't have kissed you."

No, he probably shouldn't have. But he had and she had liked it. A lot. He was ruining it by apologizing. "I didn't stop you."

"No, but that doesn't make it right."

But it felt right. So very right.

Henry glanced around the kitchen. "I work for you. I shouldn't take advantage—"

"Would you stop it?" She rose on her tiptoes and kissed him. Until she couldn't breathe. Until she couldn't take it anymore. Elisabeth tore her mouth away. "There."

"Where?"

"You can stop apologizing," she said. "Now we're even."

But as she said the words, she knew they weren't true. Henry might not be the player she imagined he was, but he sure could kiss. Suddenly the farm wasn't her only concern. She had a much bigger one—her heart.

Chapter Seven

Saturday morning, Henry stood on a street corner in downtown Berry Patch with the three Wheeler kids in tow, wishing he were anywhere but here. Portland, Prague, Paris. Parnassus would be an improvement. But no, he was on a guided tour of a small town with an eleven-year-old who didn't want to be here either, an eight-year-old who knew too much about everything and a four-year-old who had to go to the bathroom in every building they passed.

It served Henry right for kissing their sister.

All he'd wanted was a taste of Elisabeth, one kiss to kill his growing curiosity, not fuel his fantasies and make him want another kiss and another. Henry blew out a puff of air.

He waited for one of the two traffic signals in town to turn green and fought the urge to hit the crosswalk button again. Once he crossed Main Street his tour would be over. He was tempted to run, not walk, across the street and straight out of town. That would be the only way to make the adage "out of sight, out of mind" come true. He had to get the constant thoughts of Elisabeth out of his head or he was going to go crazy.

The light changed to green, and the Walk symbol illuminated. Caitlin slipped her small hand into his and glanced up at him. "I'm not supposed to cross the street without holding hands."

Abby grabbed on to his other hand. "Me, either."

Sam sneered. "I'm too old to hold hands."

"You're never too old to hold hands," Henry said, wishing that's all he would have done with Elisabeth last night. He thought the farm work would kill him. He'd been wrong. Elisabeth was the one who would do him in. Her and her kisses.

What was happening to him?

His reaction made zero sense. He'd kissed lots of women. More than he could count. But none had ever had this rock-his-world effect. He didn't like it and wanted it to stop.

"That covers downtown Berry Patch," Abby said with tour-guide hospitality after they crossed the street and stopped in front of the bistro. "Of course, the zip code covers approximately thirty miles of acreage surrounding the town, but that's mainly farms and vineyards." She glanced around. "I don't see Elisabeth so she must still be meeting with Mr. Jackson."

Sam scuffed his toe against the cement. "She's never going to sell the farm to him."

The kids had been mumbling about that all morning. "Then why is she meeting with him?" Henry asked.

Abby shrugged. "Elisabeth is too nice to say no when he calls."

Nice? Elisabeth wasn't nice. Nice girls didn't kiss the way she did.

"Maybe Elisabeth wants to marry him," Caitlin said.

The idea of Elisabeth marrying anyone left Henry feeling strangely unsettled, but it did give him an idea. If Elisabeth were kissing another man, she wouldn't be kissing him. If she weren't kissing him, Henry wouldn't be wondering when he'd get another kiss. He would be able to concentrate on farming and making life better for the Wheelers.

Sure he would. "Do you think Elisabeth likes Mr. Jackson?"

"No one likes Mr. Jackson," Abby said.

"He's a mean old man," Sam explained.

Old was a relative term when it came to kids. "How old?" Henry asked.

"Fifty, sixty," Sam said. "You know, old."

Too old for Elisabeth. Relief stole through Henry. Still, playing matchmaker wasn't such a bad idea. In fact, he tried mustering some enthusiasm: it was a good idea. Look at his success with his…friends. Look at his success with Cynthia. With the right man in the picture, Henry wouldn't feel so bad about leaving Elisabeth and her family once his month was up.

What kind of man would be good enough for her?

Someone who was the opposite of him. The realization made him feel oddly hollow, but he knew what she needed.

Someone with lots of husband potential. Who loved kids. Was handy. Knew farming. And could love her the way she deserved to be loved.

"Can we do something?" Caitlin asked.

"Mrs. Showalter is having a yard sale." Abby adjusted her glasses. "It's only two blocks away."

Caitlin beamed. "I want to go."

"Like we need any more junk." Sam shoved his hands in baggy pants' pockets. "Or have money to spend."

Henry remembered Laurel Matthews often found items for her interior decorating business at garage and yard sales. "I have a little money." Twenty dollars. Chump change to what he was used to spending. Surely that could buy something at a yard sale. "Let's go."

"If we have to," Sam said.

At Mrs. Showalter's house, the kids ran to a table full of toys. Piles and stacks of stuff lay everywhere. Henry didn't know where to start. He caught a glimpse of something white sitting on the grass. He took a closer look. A porch swing. The paint was peeling, but it looked sturdy. He checked the slats on the back. They were all there and so were chains to hang it with. The Wheeler's porch needed a swing.

Caitlin carried an old, naked baby doll in her arms. A sticker read twenty-five cents. "Can I have this?"

Ink marks covered the doll's arms and legs. A smiley-face sticker was plastered on the back of the doll's head. Talk about ugly. Not even a mother could love that hideous thing.

"Are you sure you want that doll?" he asked.

She cradled it against her chest. "I love my baby. Her name is Flower. Isn't she pretty?"

"Not as pretty as you, but you can have her."

"Thank you." Caitlin pointed to the swing. "What's that?"

"A swing for a porch."

"May I have this, please?" Abby carried a science book in her hand. "We used to have a porch swing. My mommy used to sit on it with us and we'd wait for Daddy to come in from the fields."

"What happened to the swing?" Henry asked.

"It fell apart after our parents went to heaven," Abby said. "Elisabeth was so sad."

Elisabeth always seemed a little sad. Even when she smiled, but Henry was going to fix that. She needed more in her life than working, cooking and cleaning. She needed happiness, love, a porch swing. "Do you think she would like this?"

Abby nodded.

Sam walked up. He held a videotape in his hands. "Can I get this?"

Caitlin grinned. "Henry's buying a new porch swing."

"That doesn't look new to me." Sam frowned. "It's too old and beat up."

"That will make it all the cheaper to buy," Henry said, hoping the swing and the items the kids picked out were less than twenty dollars. He did have his paycheck in his pocket, but he needed Elisabeth to cash it for him. "We can fix the swing so it looks brand-new."

Sam raised a brow. "Do you know how to do that?"

"No," Henry admitted. "But between all of us we can figure it out and surprise Elisabeth with it."

The wariness in Sam's eyes reminded Henry of Elisabeth. "Why would you buy her a swing?"

"Because it might make her smile." He picked up the swing. "Let's see if we can afford all this."

They made their way to an older lady who the kids called Mrs. Showalter. Gray curls stuck out from the bright yellow bandana she wore on her head. Large beaded earrings dangled from her ears. She wore a multicolored muumuu with large flowers on the fabric.

"How much is the porch swing, the doll, book and video?" Henry asked.

"We're going to paint the swing and give it to my sister," Caitlin added.

"That's thoughtful, dear." Mrs. Showalter added up the items on a small calculator. "Thirty dollars will cover everything."

Too much. Henry had never bargained before. Hell, this was his first time looking at a price tag. But he didn't want to disappoint the kids. "Fifteen."

Mrs. Showalter narrowed her brown eyes. "Twenty-five."

Still too high. He had one last shot. "Twenty."

She nodded once. "Sold."

The girls cheered. Sam mumbled a "whatever," but he grabbed his videotape.

Henry handed over his twenty.

"You drive a hard bargain, young man."

Satisfaction flowed through him. He'd never felt so good about buying gifts. "Thanks."

Mrs. Showalter smiled. "No, thank you."

The four of them stood around the newly purchased swing. Henry wasn't sure what to do with it. "So now we have to figure out how to get the swing back to the farm and refinished without Elisabeth finding out."

Animation lit Sam's usually sullen face. "Gabe can help us."

"There's more stuff in the back. See what I found," Gabriel Logan said, pushing a wheelbarrow full of old bricks from the backyard. He reminded Henry of a modern-day knight except he used an electric drill not a sword for his rescues. "What have you got there?"

Sam pointed to the swing. "Can you tell us how to fix the porch swing Henry bought for Elisabeth?"

Mr. Fix-It-Man set the wheelbarrow down and studied Henry. "You bought this for her?"

Henry nodded, wishing he'd watched a few of those home-improvement shows he'd glimpsed while channel surfing.

Gabriel kneeled and checked out the swing as the girls gave him hugs. "It won't take long to get this back in shape. I'd be happy to help. Anything for my Bess."

His Bess? Gabriel spoke with such affection and the look in his eyes softened.

Something clicked in Henry's mind. He didn't know anything about farms or building things or fixing machinery, but here was a man in Berry Patch who did. A man who wasn't wearing a wedding ring. A man who liked kids, too.

Gabriel Logan might just be the perfect man for Elisabeth. And the entire Wheeler family.

It would be easy for Henry to get these two together and play matchmaker. But the realization didn't bring any excitement or relief. No, the only thing it brought was a sickening feeling in his stomach and the desire to swallow a handful of antacid.

Two nights later, Henry wasn't feeling better. It wasn't his stomach this time, but insomnia. He couldn't sleep. He also couldn't move thanks to Ruff and the nameless gray cat using Henry as its own personal mattress. Henry was not going to miss sharing a twin-size bed with them when he was gone.

He wasn't going to miss all the work it took to winterize the farm, either. At least he was no longer making so many mistakes. Or rather, not such noticeable ones.

The one area he was succeeding in was fairy godfathering. It was working for everyone but Elisabeth. The kids loved their yard sale gifts and the porch swing was coming along with Gabe's help.

Gabe.

Henry liked Gabe. Respected him, too. The guy was working miracles with the porch swing and teaching them a thing or two about carpentry. But woodworking wasn't the only thing Gabe knew. He also knew women.

Forget about fixing him up with Elisabeth.

Gabe Logan was too much like Henry, a rogue not a hero, and that wouldn't do for Elisabeth. She deserved better. No, she deserved the best.

But with Henry's job, he didn't have time to meet all the single men in Berry Patch and find the right one for Elisabeth. He would have to forgo matchmaking. The decision brought a rush of relief. Less work for him, he rationalized.

Cymbals crashed. Trombones played. And the plucking of strings filled the air. It sounded like an orchestra. But at this hour?

Henry scooted the gray cat off his chest and sat, careful not to bump his head on the lower bunk. He listened to the classical music. An odd sound considering he never heard music being played at the Wheelers' house. Not on a CD player, not on the radio. The only time was when Caitlin watched one of her kid videos.

The music piqued Henry's curiosity. Maybe Abby was analyzing a composer. Maybe there was more to Sam than baggy pants and a bad attitude. No, it had to be Abby.

Henry slid out of bed and headed downstairs. The only lights were the dingy brass candlestick wall sconces above each end of the fireplace mantel. The soft glow provided enough light to see into the living room.

Halfway down the stairs, Henry froze.

Elisabeth sat on the couch. She wore a ratty light-colored robe. Her bare feet beat in time to the music. Her hair was loose and tousled. Sexy. He should go back to bed before she saw him.

He did a double take. Her eyes were closed. She had a serene Mona Lisa smile on her face. She swayed gently to the music. So lovely. He sat on the stairs and watched.

When a harp played its first note, so did Elisabeth. She plucked and strummed at a non-existent harp with the skill and precision of a master. The play of emotions across her face mesmerized Henry. He'd never seen such passion, such concentration, such…contentment. The expressions made him want to find a way to make her feel this way every single day, not just in the middle of the night, alone in the dark, air-harping.

This was a private moment, and he was intruding. Henry didn't care. He was staying until she made him move. This new side of Elisabeth mesmerized him.

As the music continued to play, so did she. Not once did she open her eyes. She sat with such grace. Her elbows up and out, her thumbs up and her fingers curved. Her feet pressed make-believe pedals. He wondered what she thought about, what she imagined as she played.

The song ended. Elisabeth rose from the couch and bowed. Henry clapped. A little too enthusiastically before he caught himself.

Too late.

The light on the end table next to her turned on. Damn, he'd forgotten about the clapper.

Elisabeth's eyelids sprang open. She stared at him. Her eyes sparkled. Her cheeks flushed. "What are you doing up?"

"I couldn't sleep." He climbed down the rest of the stairs. "I heard music and wanted to see what was going on."

"I'm sorry."

"Don't be sorry," he said. "It was worth getting up to see you play."

"I wasn't playing, only pretending." She sounded embarrassed.

"Or practicing?" he offered.

The color on her cheeks deepened. She sat on the couch.

He sat next to her. "I didn't know you were a musician."

"I'm not," she said quickly. "I mean, I used to be. But not any longer."

"You seem to enjoy it."

"It's okay." She clasped her hands together. "I started playing when I was six. An older woman in town asked my father if she could teach me. I think she felt sorry for us because my mother had died."

"Why did you stop playing?"

"No time. Plus there wasn't a reason to keep at it. No orchestras in Berry Patch. There are weddings and wineries, but it's easier to use a folk harp for those gigs. You could do it with a pedal harp, too, but it's not as easy to cart around."

Her answers sounded too pat. Too much like excuses. Had she used them to justify not playing the harp? He would hate it if that were true.

"Where's your harp?" he asked.

A muscle ticked in her jaw. "I…I sold it."

"Why?"

"We needed the money." She sighed. "The Deere broke down right before harvest two years ago. The Suburban needed an overhaul. A hundred other things."

The light in her eyes dimmed. He wanted to bring it back. "Elisabeth—"

"It's no big deal. Really." She spoke quickly as if trying to convince herself. "It's not as if I was going to make a career out of playing the harp and travel the world performing with all the great orchestras."

"Was that your dream?"

"Yes. I mean, once it was." She tilted her chin. "But not now."

She might have thought so, but Henry wasn't convinced. "There's nothing wrong with dreams."

She shrugged.

"You've given up so much of your life already to the farm and your siblings, you can't give up your dreams, too. It's not too late—"

"It is too late. I have the kids and the farm and my job."

"You could sell the farm to Mr. Jackson."

"Never." Her eyes darkened. "This is the only home my family has ever known. I won't take that away from them. No matter what it takes."

"Even if it's not what you want to do."

"It's what I have to do. I don't deserve to have my dreams come true. If it wasn't for me, my dad and stepmother would still be alive." The words tumbled out. Her eyes widened once she realized what she'd revealed.

Henry needed to proceed slowly, cautiously. "I thought they were in a car accident."

"They were, but I'm the one who convinced them to go out on a date. If it weren't for me, they would still be alive. My brother and sisters would have parents. The farm wouldn't be struggling so badly. Neither would we."

"It isn't your fault, Elisabeth," Henry explained. He wanted to take away her pain, her guilt. "You weren't driving the car. You weren't even there. It was an accident."

She stared at the pictures on the mantel. "Caitlin wouldn't sleep through the night. I'd come home for the weekend and my stepmother was so tired. She needed a break so I told them to go on a date and I would watch the kids. They did, and they never came home again."

"They might have gone out anyway. Or had all the kids with them. Or a million other scenarios." Henry wanted to shake some sense into her. He knew what this kind of guilt could do to a person. "You can't continue blaming yourself."

Tears glimmered in her eyes. "How can I not blame myself?

His heart ached for her.

He'd been there himself. Except he'd been a lot older than twenty-one and he didn't have a baby to take care of and a brother and a sister and a farm. She would have had no time for herself. No time to mourn for the loss of her parents. Only time to blame herself. And give up her own life and dreams to make up for something that wasn't her fault.

"Things happen for no reason. Sometimes good things, sometimes bad. And that can be hard to accept, especially when those things are beyond our control."

She said nothing. But her pain, her despair, tore at him. He never opened up, never let anyone get too close, but just this once he needed to. For Elisabeth.

"After my parents were killed in the plane crash, I blamed myself." This wasn't easy for him to admit. He took a deep breath. "I was supposed to be on their flight, but I was too hungover and called them at the airport to tell them I would be taking a later flight. They were disappointed in me, but said they would wait. I told them it wasn't necessary. I didn't relish being trapped on a transatlantic flight listening to them tell me how I wasn't living up to their expectations. But I realized that if I hadn't been so selfish, if I had told them to wait, they wouldn't have been on that flight. They wouldn't have died."

Elisabeth's face lightened. "So you know."

"I know."

Her gaze met his. "How did you get through it?"

"I didn't at first. The guilt. The grief." Knowing he would never be able to gain his parents' love. "I spent my time partying. Until my friends stepped in. Laurel and Brett Matthews and Cynthia Sterling. A few others. They got me through it. Saved me." And he would do whatever it took to repay them for their friendship and ensure their happiness.

"You're lucky to have them," Elisabeth said. "I don't—didn't—have many friends to rely on. Theresa was great, but I was engaged when it happened, and my ex-fiancé didn't understand. He didn't even try."

"The guy must have been an idiot."

The corners of her mouth lifted. "That's what Theresa said. She's a good friend."

"Yes, she is. And smart." Henry held Elisabeth's hand. Engaged so young. Too young. No wonder it didn't last. And to have lost her parents, too. "Does Theresa think you were to blame?"

"No."

"Neither do I," he said. "So you're the only one we need to convince."

Her eyes darkened. "It's not going to happen."

"Try to accept it."

She sat silent. At least she hadn't said no. That was a start. Henry would take it. "Say, 'I'm not to blame.'"

"I—I…"

Tears fell from Elisabeth's eyes. He covered her hand with his. "Try again."

She exhaled loudly. "I—I'm not to blame."

"Was that so hard?" he asked.

"Yes."

"It gets easier."

"I doubt that."

He smiled to encourage her. "Keep saying it and you'll see."

"I'll try." She rubbed her eyes. "I'm sorry for crying. I know guys hate tears."

Henry wanted to get her ex-fiancé alone in a small dark room and make him cry. He put his arm around Elisabeth and gave her a squeeze. "Everyone needs a good cry. Even guys. And it's a lot cheaper than therapy."

"How do you do it?" She gazed up at him and he felt as if he could lose himself in her eyes. "How can you make me feel so good when we're talking about something so serious?"

Warmth settled in the center of his chest. He found himself scooting toward her instead of away. "It's a gift."

"Thanks for sharing it with me."

Elisabeth hugged him. The fresh scent of her soap and shampoo filled his nostrils. He wanted to capture the fragrance in a bottle and spray it on his pillow. Her hair tickled his face and he wanted to run his fingers through the long, silky strands. She felt so soft and perfect in his arms. Her breasts pressed against his chest and heat spread through him.

Henry relished this shared moment. This hug. Her.

He wanted to kiss her.

With a pulse-pounding certainty, he knew he couldn't. He couldn't cross that line.

She didn't need his kisses; she needed his shoulder. A friend. He knew how to handle friends. He was good with his friends.

Elisabeth let go. A chill shivered through him, but her trusting smile reassured Henry. He had made the right choice. The only choice.

He caressed her cheek. "Anytime, Elisabeth. Anytime."

And he meant it.

Chapter Eight

"Kitty, kitty," Caitlin called. "Time to eat."

The fat, gray cat didn't come, but Henry filled the stainless steel bowl with food anyway. The cat would be hungry sooner or later.

He was helping Caitlin with her chores while Elisabeth cooked dinner. Anything to keep him out of the kitchen and away from her.

Henry needed space.

He was getting too close to Elisabeth. Their midnight encounter two nights ago had only been the beginning. Working together, living together. He couldn't turn around without catching a glimpse of her. And if he didn't see Elisabeth, he was thinking about her. That didn't seem…right.

Not when he was only her friend.

Henry had to keep reminding himself of that. But it was the truth. He was nothing more than the Wheelers' farmhand, friend, fairy godfather. And when the time came to leave, he was out of here.

Caitlin pouted. "Where is that cat?"

"Maybe if the cat had a name, he would come," Henry suggested.

"He has a name," she said. "Cat."

Henry chuckled. "I meant a name like Caitlin or Henry or Flower."

"How about Kitty?" she suggested.

"Good idea, but that name is a lot like Cat." Henry rubbed his chin. "How about Ritz?"

"I love Ritz crackers. So does Elisabeth."

He'd been thinking more along the lines of the Ritz Hotel, but crackers worked. Especially if Elisabeth liked them. No. Her likes didn't matter. Not to him.

"Come, Ritz." As Caitlin called the new name, Henry shook the bowl of dry food as added incentive. "Dinnertime, Ritz."

The no-longer nameless cat came running as fast as his too-small-for-his-large-body legs could carry him.

Caitlin's mouth formed a perfect *O*. "Ritz likes his name."

"Yes, he does."

"I like you," she said.

Henry ruffled her blond curls. "I like you, too, princess."

"Would you be my daddy?

He froze.

"Please."

Henry was at a loss for words. Instinct told him to pack his bag and leave. Forget about packing. He didn't need any of that stuff.

She tugged on his hand. "Will you be my daddy, Henry?"

A ten-carat diamond lump formed in his throat. He swallowed around it. "Do you want me to be the daddy when we play house?"

"Yes, but I also want you to be my daddy all the time. The other kids have mommies and daddies. I just have Elisabeth." Caitlin scratched Ritz's head and the cat purred as loud as a tractor engine. "All the princesses have daddies. Ariel, Jasmine, Belle, Sleeping Beauty."

"What about Snow White and Cinderella?" As two little lines formed above the bridge of Caitlin's nose, Henry brushed aside his own question. "You have a daddy."

"But he's in heaven. You're here."

Henry couldn't deny her four-year-old logic, but he had to be logical himself. He would never be good enough. He could never be the type of man someone would look up to and call dad. Not only wasn't he father material, he didn't want to be a dad. He was too selfish, too fond of his adventures and indulgences, too determined to get his own way. His own parents hadn't been the best of role models, but Henry was pretty sure being a parent meant learning to give up control as much as it meant learning to take responsibility. And he was no good at either one.

He winced. Well, he liked some responsibilities. He liked making his friends happy. But being a father didn't allow you to make friends happy. Being a father didn't allow you to pick and choose. If fathers made a mistake, it was a big deal. "But I'm not a daddy. I'm…Henry."

Her lower lip quivered. Oh man, he didn't want her to cry. She was just a little girl who wanted to be loved. He ignored the tug on his heart. "What if I became your fairy godfather instead?"

"What does a fairy godfather do?" she asked.

"He makes sure you are happy and smiling all the time."

She grinned. "You already do that. You bought me Flower and played vet with me. Oh, and colored."

"Then I'm one step ahead of the game," he said.

"Will you still call me princess?"

"Of course, princess." He emphasized the last word. "Okay?"

As she nodded, her curls bobbed up and down. "Okay."

But it wasn't. Henry felt like he'd dodged a bullet. Three of them. But Caitlin was happy and he was relieved. A fairy godfather or a real godfather he could be.

A real father?

Forget it.

I'm not to blame.

Over the next few days, the words became Elisabeth's mantra. She wanted, and was trying hard, to believe them. The words gave her a peace about her parents' deaths and a sense of freedom she hadn't thought possible. And it was all due to Henry.

Thinking about him brought a welcome smile to her face. She couldn't help it. He was thoughtful and caring and hardworking.

He was also becoming a…problem.

She glanced at the clock on her dashboard and stepped on the gas. The engine spurted. She pressed on the gas pedal again. Finally the Suburban accelerated.

She couldn't deny he was gorgeous. Any breathing female would be attracted to him. But Elisabeth's growing feelings for him went beyond the physical and that bothered her. A lot. She'd lost a fiancé over her siblings.

She would never get involved with a man who didn't want kids. Not that she wanted to get involved with Henry, she reminded herself.

She didn't.

But she was getting attached. So were the kids. She didn't want to think about what would happen when Henry left, but she had to.

He would be leaving. Just as soon as Manny returned.

She had to prepare herself and the kids for his departure. They would have to get used to an empty space at the table again. They would have to give Ruff extra love and attention. Ritz would be back to sleeping on top of her. They would have to put a radio in the bathroom to take the place of Henry's singing in the shower.

Maybe it would be good if she distanced herself and the kids from Henry. But how?

Caitlin tagged after Henry as much as Ruff did. Abby sought him out to help her with homework or some advanced subject she'd decided to study for fun. Sam pretended not to care, but Elisabeth noticed he watched Henry and not with the same distrust he used to show. She even looked forward to having coffee with him during their breaks.

Distance wasn't possible.

Elisabeth stopped the car in front of the barn. She jerked the parking brake into place, yanked the keys out of the ignition and jumped out of the Suburban. If she hurried, she could get the feed unloaded and a chicken in the Crock-Pot for dinner.

Ruff barked.

"Home from work?" Henry asked from behind her.

The rich sound of his voice sent a shiver of pleasure down her spine. Darn. She didn't want to react to his voice. To him. Not when she was already missing him and he wasn't even gone. Elisabeth pushed a strand of hair that had fallen out of her ponytail behind her ear. "Yes."

"A little early for you."

It wasn't a question. Elisabeth hadn't known Henry paid attention to her schedule. His interest flattered her. Made her feel warm and tingly inside.

Stop it.

It shouldn't mean anything. She hated that it did. Elisabeth opened the tailgate so she could remove the two fifty-pound bags of feed.

She untied her stained apron and tossed it into the SUV. Bill Tucker's two-year-old son had squirted a bottle of ketchup all over the table and her, but she didn't want to get it dirtier. "A waitress is sick so Kathy needs me to work the dinner shift, too. I needed to do a few things here first."

"That's going to be a long day for you."

She struggled to pull one of the feed bags out. "I've done it before."

"Let me take that," he said.

She appreciated his offer, but she didn't need the help. She wouldn't rely on him any more than she had to. "Thanks, but I can do it."

"I know you can." Henry picked up the bag without any effort. "But I want to help."

She worked on removing the next one.

"Do you want me to get the kids from school and watch them for you?"

Baby-sitting was a long way from wanting to have children of his own, but his offer made her wonder if the kids were softening his views on having a family. "Theresa's going to do it. She picked Caitlin up from preschool and will get Sam and Abby later, but thanks."

"I'll do it some other time." Henry sounded eager as he picked up the other bag, and her heart danced with possibility. "What about this weekend? You could go out."

"Out where?" she asked.

"Out on a date."

He was offering to baby-sit so she could go out with another man? Ouch. She needed more than distance from Henry; she needed a reality check.

"I don't date." Ick. She sounded like a pathetic, shriveled-up spinster. Might as well hand him a list with all her flaws and fears. "I mean, I rarely date. The kids and all. Theresa is always wanting to fix me up with someone, but I hate blind dates as much as I hate matchmaking."

Henry stared at her. "So you're not looking for Mr. Right?"

"I'm not looking for Mr. Anything." But as she said the words she got the funny feeling she was looking at Mr. Right. Her mouth went dry.

"Instead of a date, you and Theresa could hit the town for a girls' night out."

"We haven't done that in a long time." Too long, Elisabeth realized.

"You could have fun," Henry said.

"Why are you so interested in my having fun?"

Henry widened his stance. "You work harder than anyone I know. You need a break if only for a few hours. Away from the bistro, the farm, the kids."

"Three kids can be a lot of work. Think you can handle them?"

"Yes." Confidence laced the word. "Caitlin goes to bed early. Abby likes to read. Sam and I can figure something out or just talk."

Elisabeth raised a brow. "Talk to Sam?"

"Maybe we'll watch videos."

Henry did know the kids pretty well. He was good with them. As long as cooking wasn't involved she wouldn't worry about their safety. Not with Sam there. Abby was mature for her age. And Caitlin would describe to Elisabeth everything down to the smallest detail that happened while she was gone. Maybe this would work. And she did need time away. Not from the farm or the kids. But from Henry. "I'll talk to Theresa."

"Do," Henry encouraged. "Ask her about this Friday night."

"I will." Her feet dragged on the way to the house, and she glanced back. The way he was looking at her made her heart beat triple time. "And Henry. Thank you."

A dazzling smile lit up his face. "My pleasure."

Great. He was pleased because she had agreed to go out for a night. Without him. She'd wanted some distance and she'd gotten it. So why wasn't she happy about it?

Friday—girls' night out—arrived. Henry was prepared. Elisabeth had cashed his second paycheck for him this morning. He'd spent his entire first check on supplies for the nearly finished porch swing and a few extra treats for Elisabeth, but this week he had money left over after shopping for tonight's activities—a tea party for Caitlin, a build your own ice-cream-sundae science experiment for Abby and a rented video game system for Sam.

Almost time. Henry was itching to get started. He rubbed his palms together.

The Wheelers' fairy godfather had found his groove.

It was all he could do not to write out an itinerary for Elisabeth and Theresa's girls' night out. He realized doing so would be overstepping the bounds, but it felt odd not being able to insure her a good time.

"How do I look?" Elisabeth asked as she walked down the stairs.

Henry's breath caught in his throat. He was used to seeing her wear jeans or her waitress uniform or a Sunday church dress or her bathrobe. But all dressed up…

Damn, she cleaned up well.

Her powder-blue button down stretch shirt matched her eyes and accentuated her breasts. Her above-the-knee, khaki skirt made her legs look longer. Good thing he'd decided not to play matchmaker. She didn't need one; she needed a bodyguard. Henry swallowed. Hard.

"You're stunning." He forced the words from his dry throat.

Elisabeth glanced at the brown mules on her feet and her cheeks reddened. "Thanks."

"You're wearing makeup."

She touched her cheek. "Is it too much?"

"No, it's just right. And your hair, too," he said. "The men of Berry Patch had better watch out."

Her sparkling gaze met his. "You're so sweet."

She wouldn't think he was so sweet if she had any clue about the images running through his mind. Images of him slowly unbuttoning her shirt and slipping her skirt over the curve of her hips.

A car door slammed. Time to pull himself together. Not only for his sake, but for the kids' sakes, too.

"You and Theresa have fun tonight," he said.

Elisabeth picked up her sweater from the back of the couch. "Theresa couldn't make it tonight."

"Then who—"

A knock sounded. Henry opened the front door and wanted to slam it shut.

Gabriel Logan stood with a wide grin on his face and a bouquet of colorful flowers in his hands. "How's it going, Henry?"

Baby-sitting was going well. The tea party had been a success as well as the ice-cream sundae experiments. He'd played house with the girls and handled being "daddy" without suffering an anxiety attack or needing a therapist. Caitlin had fallen asleep on the couch at eight o'clock. Abby at nine. Both were tucked safely in their beds. Henry had checked on them twice. Ruff slept at his feet. Ritz was curled up on the recliner. All Henry needed now was for Elisabeth to get home.

"Yes." Sam raised his hands in the air. "I win."

"Not again." Henry tossed his control pad on the coffee table and glanced at the clock on the VCR. 10:06 p.m. Only eight minutes had passed since the last time he'd looked.

Why wasn't Elisabeth home yet? Dinner didn't take that long. And there wasn't much nightlife in Berry Patch.

"Why do you keep checking the clock?" Sam asked.

"Wondering when your sister might be home."

"Don't worry about her." Sam stuck a new game cartridge into the video game system. "She's with Gabe. He'll take care of her."

That's what Henry was afraid of. Knowing Gabe Logan's reputation, he could find plenty of ways to keep Elisabeth entertained. Henry wrung his hands.

Sam sat next to him. "Are you ready to play the snowboarding game?"

Anticipation filled his voice. Sam wasn't so bad once you got past the apathy and the sneer and his being eleven. His vocabulary even included other words besides "whatever" and "sucks." Not to mention he had amazing hand-eye coordination. Henry needed something to take his mind off Elisabeth. Maybe a different game would do the trick. "Sure, but I've never played that one."

"It's not hard," Sam said. "Even you will be able to figure it out."

"Even me?"

The corners of Sam's mouth edged up.

Henry picked up his control pad and readied himself as if he were a sharpshooter from the Old West. "I'll show you."

By the time midnight rolled around, Sam was asleep in bed and Henry had played enough video games to give him carpal tunnel syndrome. Elisabeth still wasn't home.

He didn't like it.

He didn't like the way he kept glancing at the clock.

He didn't like the way he wanted to call the police station and make sure there hadn't been accident.

She was his friend. His boss. That's why he was concerned about her. There wasn't any other reason. Henry picked up toys and put them in the basket. He wasn't much of a housekeeper, but he had to do something to keep himself from imagining Elisabeth lying on the side of the road or on the side of Gabe. Henry carried the popcorn bowl into the kitchen, dumped the half-popped kernels into the garbage and washed the bowl.

Why hadn't he been the one to go out with her? He could have shown her a better time than Gabriel Logan.

The answer hit Henry: Sam, Abby and Caitlin. If Henry hadn't suggested her going out, Elisabeth would be at home. With him.

Damn.

Henry tossed the dish towel on the counter. He had only himself to blame. He walked back into the living room and plopped onto the couch.

A car pulled to a stop outside. A two-ton weight fell off his shoulders. Now if he could just see her.

Henry watched the clock. A minute passed. And another. And yet another. The seconds dragged. Each minute seemed like an hour.

What was going on out there?

It didn't take that long to say good-night. Unless...

Henry sprang to his feet. He was halfway to the door when it opened, and Elisabeth stepped inside.

"What's going on?" she asked.

"I, uh, was going to let Ritz out."

She hung her purse on a hook by the door. "He has a cat door."

"I forgot."

Henry studied her. The circles under her eyes were less noticeable. The rosy glow on her cheeks made her look younger. She was smiling and radiant. It made him feel great, that he was doing the right thing by telling her to go out. Even if it was with Gabe.

"How were the kids?" she asked.

"Great."

She arched a brow. "Even Sam?"

"Especially Sam. We played video games after the girls went to bed," Henry admitted. "How was your date?"

His jaw clenched. He hadn't meant to ask, but he was...curious. He sat on the couch.

"It wasn't really a date."

Good news. Great, actually. Though he realized it shouldn't have mattered. "So what did you do?"

"We drove to Dundee for dinner. Then we went to The Vine to hear a new band." She sat next to Henry. "It was nice. Gabe treated me like a princess."

Damn and double damn. "You deserve to be treated like a princess."

By me. Not him.

"Did he kiss you?" The words rushed out before Henry could stop them.

"Gabe kisses everyone."

So did Henry. Aw, hell.

His gut told him Gabriel Logan was not the man for Elisabeth. Henry had already decided not to play matchmaker so finding someone else wasn't an alternative. What else could he do? He rubbed his chin.

"You okay?" she asked.

"Fine," he said. "I'm just fine."

"Me, too." Her smile reached her eyes. "Thank you for suggesting I go out. I needed it."

"I'm happy you had fun." But he wasn't happy. Not really. And that bugged him. He was her friend, her fairy godfather, and he should be happy she'd enjoyed herself. She had needed tonight. She needed more. And if it turned out she needed Gabe—

She leaned forward and kissed Henry. On the lips. Hard.

She tasted like wine and chocolate. His heart slammed against his chest and the blood rushed from his head.

Wanting this was wrong. He didn't care. Because it felt right. And he wanted more—more of her kisses and more of her.

He was crossing the line. Hell, he'd jumped without a thought. But she had been the one to initiate the kiss. Not him. This was her doing. Not his.

And he was enjoying it. A lot.

Still he held back. Somehow he managed not to touch her anywhere except on the lips. It wasn't nearly enough, but that was all he dared.

Achingly, the kiss came to an end.

A slow smile spread over her face. "I thought so."

He could barely breathe, let alone think. "Thought what?"

"That you kissed better than Gabe." She rose from the couch. "Good night, Henry."

He sat there, stunned.

There was nothing good about tonight.

Henry had left the evening up to fate, but Elisabeth had grabbed the reins. The result? Chaos. She'd turned everything upside down by looking so gorgeous. By going out with the flower-toting Gabe and kissing him. And by ending the night kissing Henry.

He wanted to be in control, but he didn't want to take responsibility. Tonight proved he couldn't control Elisabeth, and he couldn't help feeling responsible for her, either.

Henry didn't like it.

He was supposed to be her fairy godfather, but that's the last thing he felt like right now.

All he wanted to do was take her in his arms and kiss her. He wanted to shower her with diamonds and pearls and sapphires. He wanted to show her how wonderful life could be without all her responsibilities.

But wanting those things made no sense.

Henry wasn't here for the long haul. He didn't believe in the long haul. He wasn't the man she thought he was. He wasn't even close. He would never be good enough for her. He would never be the type of man she loved.

No, not loved. Wanted.

And that hurt. More than he thought possible.

Chapter Nine

The next day, Elisabeth stared out the window at the passing scenery. Early morning chores, a car that wouldn't start and the Saturday lunch shift at the bistro had worn her out. Not to mention a restless night.

She had dreamed Henry was staying on the farm. Not only until Manny returned, but forever. In her dream she'd been euphoric at the news.

Too bad there wasn't room in her life for fantasies, daydreams and romance. Her shoulders sagged.

"You okay?" Theresa asked.

"I'm okay." Elisabeth straightened. "Thanks for the ride home. I hope Gabe fixed the Suburban."

"He was working on it when I left to pick you up. If it can be fixed, he'll do it, but the Suburban is almost as old as you are. You're going to need a new car."

She needed a new brain.

No wonder she was dreaming about Henry after

the way she'd kissed him last night. Kissing him the first time had been bad enough, but twice? She couldn't even blame it on the wine; she'd only had one glass.

The fault lay completely with her.

She'd kissed him only to prove she'd magnified his kiss to mythic proportions because she hadn't been kissed in such a long time. After Gabe's pleasant goodnight kiss with no zings or tingles or fireworks, Elisabeth had figured Henry's kiss would be the same—nice, but uneventful. She would be able to distance herself mentally and forget about his kisses and him.

She'd been wrong. He hadn't even taken her in his arms, but his lips against hers were all she needed to realize she hadn't blown his kiss out of proportion. To be honest, kissing him had been better than she remembered. Much better. Elisabeth leaned her head back against the seat. "I need a new everything."

Theresa popped a CD in the player and a romantic ballad played over the car speakers. "Does that include a new farmhand?"

"Henry's doing better." If only he was as great at farming as he was at kissing they could turn the farm around. "He's not making as many mistakes. Though the other day when I asked him to bring a chicken for dinner he thought he had to kill one." Her insides had melted when she saw him holding on to a hen and petting it, an axe on the ground outside the chicken coop. "Luckily he couldn't do it. He was so relieved when I showed him the freezer where we kept the frozen chicken."

"Henry's a great guy," Theresa said.

"How would you know?"

"You haven't been complaining about him. You haven't really talked about Henry at all." Theresa glanced over at her. "What's up with that?"

"Nothing."

"You like him."

Like didn't describe how Elisabeth felt about Henry. She wasn't sure what word did. "He works for me."

"That's an excuse, not a reason." Theresa tapped the steering wheel to the beat of the music. "If you don't like him, why are you blushing?"

"I'm…I'm hot."

"And bothered?"

Elisabeth wasn't about to answer that.

Theresa continued. "I don't blame you for feeling that way because he's perfect for you."

"I thought *you* liked him."

She shrugged. "I would never stand in the way of true love."

"True what?"

"Love." Theresa winked. "Elisabeth plus Henry equals true love."

If only…no, Elisabeth couldn't think about that. "You'll only be disappointed." Elisabeth hadn't realized she'd spoken out loud.

"A girl can dream, can't she?" Theresa turned the car onto the dirt driveway leading to the farm. "There's nothing wrong with one friend wanting to see another friend live happily ever after."

"Fairy-tale endings aren't real."

"Just wait," Theresa said. "Your once-upon-a-time is closer than you think."

Theresa had lost it. Still the idea of loving and being loved appealed to Elisabeth in a way it hadn't in years.

Not since Toby. Yet at the same time it frightened her. "And you think Henry is a part of it?"

"You said it, not me." Theresa parked her car next to Gabe's truck. The hood to the Suburban was raised.

Not a good sign. Elisabeth had wanted it to be an easy fix. She couldn't afford anything serious to be wrong. But the way her luck was running…

Elisabeth slid out of the car and prepared herself for the worst. Caitlin, Abby and Henry greeted her. The girls jumped up and down and giggled. Elisabeth had never had a welcome home like this. Henry's influence? Or was something wrong?

"We have a surprise for you," Caitlin said. "Close your eyes."

Elisabeth did as she was told. "Now what?"

Small fingers clasped her right hand.

"Don't peek," Abby said. "We'll lead you there."

As Elisabeth took a step, a larger hand took hold of her left hand. Tingles raced up her arm and down to the tips of her ugly white shoes.

"Don't worry," Henry whispered. "We won't lead you astray."

His warm breath caressed her neck. Being led astray didn't sound so bad at this moment.

Her shoes crunched on the gravel. "Where are we going?"

"Be patient," Caitlin ordered in the same tone Elisabeth sometimes used with her.

They released her hands.

"You can open your eyes," Abby said.

Elisabeth did. A soft gasp escaped her lips.

"Surprise," everyone shouted.

She covered her mouth with her hands. "This can't be our house."

"It is," Caitlin said, clapping.

On closer inspection Elisabeth knew it was, but somehow the front porch had been magically transformed from rundown and neglected to new and beautiful like a layout from a home and garden magazine.

A sparkling white swing hung from chains. The broken slats on the railing had been repaired. A flower basket had been hung and potted plants of different sizes had been added.

Sam was there. Gabe and Theresa, too.

Abby bit her lip. "Do you like it?"

Elisabeth gave her sister a reassuring squeeze. "I love it. So much. It's beautiful. But who did this?"

Smiles lit up their faces. "We did."

"Henry bought the swing and supplies," Abby said.

Sam stepped forward. "Gabe showed us how to refinish it and fix up the porch."

"Theresa did the plants," Caitlin added.

Tears stung Elisabeth's eyes and she blinked them away. She ran her fingers along the edge of the porch rail. The front of the house hadn't looked this good in years. "I still can't believe this is our house."

"This is so great." Theresa rubbed her eyes. "It reminds me of the Learning Channel show *While You Were Out.*"

"This is better." Happiness bubbled inside Elisabeth. Not because of the porch, but because of the people who did this for her. "All this work. Thank you doesn't seem like enough."

"A hug would work," Abby, ever practical, suggested.

Elisabeth grinned. "I can do that."

She hugged each of the kids. Theresa, too. Gabriel was next.

"We all helped," he whispered. "But this was Henry's idea."

Henry?

Once again, she'd been surprised by the unpredictable Henry. Emotion surged through her. "You shouldn't have gone to so much trouble, Henry."

"I wish I could have done more," he said.

The warmth of his smile blanketed her, made her feel cherished and special. A hug didn't seem an adequate gesture of thanks. But she couldn't risk anything more. Not with her heart pounding and her gaze focused on his lips.

Elisabeth forced herself to look away. As she wrapped her arms around him, his scent intoxicated her. It felt so good to touch him, to hold him. "Thank you."

She waited for him to hug back. He stiffened instead. As her chest tightened, she ignored the disappointment his reaction brought and stepped back.

Henry still had a grin on his face. He acted as if nothing were wrong. She didn't understand. Had she imagined the awkwardness? Was she being hypersensitive? Was she afraid to enjoy the moment? She wasn't used to people doing things for her. For the first time in almost four years, someone had. Maybe that was it.

He motioned to the swing. "Why don't you try it?"

As the swing went back and forth, she felt like a kid again, carefree, safe. It was a good feeling. She remembered swinging with her mother and later her stepmother. The spot next to Elisabeth was now empty, and so was a spot in her heart. No one had been able to fill it. No one had wanted to try. For the first time in a long while, Elisabeth wished someone would.

She stared at Henry and sighed.

"What's wrong?" Henry didn't like the kids' sad faces as they sat at the dinner table waiting to be served. Strange, considering today had been such a good day.

Sam grimaced. "Can't you smell it?"

Henry inhaled. The awful aroma made him wrinkle his nose. "What is that?"

"Dinner," Elisabeth answered as she stood in front of the stove and stirred one of the pots.

"Liver and onions," Abby added.

Caitlin pouted. "I'm not eating it."

"Me, either," Sam said.

"You'll eat it." Elisabeth placed full plates in front of each of them. "It's good for you."

Henry had never seen something so unappetizing in all his life. Pâté was made from liver, but this? No way could this dish be good for anyone. "I'm not that hungry."

"I'm not hungry," Sam echoed.

Elisabeth sat. "There are children starving all over the world who would be happy to eat this."

"Let's FedEx it to them," Abby murmured. "I'd rather starve. A person can survive without food. Water, however, is critical."

Henry bit back a chuckle. Abby was so precocious and adorable. He wondered what she would be when she grew up. A scientist, a doctor, a CEO?

"It's not that bad," Elisabeth said.

As she took a bite, he glimpsed a slight grimace as she chewed. "Do you actually like this?" he asked.

She drank half her glass of milk. "My stepmother used to make it."

He noticed she didn't answer his question. Finally, something he didn't like about her—the way she prepared liver and onions. Not that he would like it prepared any way, but he wasn't going to think about that.

Sam slumped. "I didn't like it when Mom made it and hers was better."

Elisabeth drew her lips into a thin line. "Just eat."

Not one of the kids picked up a fork. Henry had always felt the need to support Elisabeth, but not in this instance. Backing her up would be something a father would do. Taking the "mother's" side. He didn't want to give the kids the wrong impression. Especially Caitlin. Besides it would be hypocritical of him when he wasn't about to eat the dinner, either.

"Ruff wouldn't eat this," Sam said.

Elisabeth sighed. "Yes, he would."

"Why don't we find out?" Henry suggested. They all needed to have more fun, especially Elisabeth. And if it kept them from having to eat the meal, that would be an added bonus. "We can do an experiment like we read about in your science book, Abby."

Elisabeth frowned. "We're not going to waste good food."

"We aren't," Sam muttered.

"What's our hypothesis?" Henry asked.

"That Ruff will not eat the food," Abby said.

"Good," Henry said. "Our assumptions?"

"Ruff has taste buds," Abby offered.

"The food is inedible," Sam said.

Elisabeth said nothing, but her eyes were watchful.

"I will perform the experiment." Henry scooped up

a forkfull of the dinner and placed it on the floor. "Come here, boy."

Ruff trotted over. He sniffed the food and gobbled it down.

Elisabeth tilted her chin. "Told you so."

"What are the conclusions, Abby?" Henry asked.

"We have not only disproved our hypothesis, but one of our assumptions," Abby explained. "Ruff does not have any taste buds."

Sam grinned. "Good one, sis."

Abby beamed.

"She's convinced me," Elisabeth said. "You don't have to eat it."

The kids cheered. Henry fought the urge to join them. He didn't want to be rude and hurt Elisabeth.

A smile tugged at the corners of her mouth. "So what should we do now?"

"Food fight?" Henry suggested.

The kids leaned over the table toward Elisabeth. Their eyes widened with anticipation.

"No." It was only one word, but her tone said it all. "Before you complain, what about dinner at the Burger Basket? Gabe said the Suburban was as good as new. We can find out if he's right."

"Burger Basket is almost as good as a food fight," Sam said.

"I want a chocolate milkshake," Caitlin said.

"This is going to ruin our budget," Abby added.

"No, it won't." Henry pulled out Elisabeth's chair for her. "Dinner is my treat."

She looked at him. "You don't have to take us out."

He didn't. He wasn't her husband or their father or anybody's provider. But he was her friend. He could do this much. He wanted to do this much for them. For her.

It was only dinner.

At the Burger Basket, not *Chez Panisse*.

He was, after all, their fairy godfather. "I want to."

"Then you have first dibs on the swing tonight," Elisabeth said.

As long as he could have it all to himself. Because if he sat on the swing with her, if he stared long enough into her caring blue eyes, he might see a reflection of the man she wanted. The man he could never be.

Sitting on the porch swing, Elisabeth gazed at the millions of stars twinkling in the dark night sky. Today had been perfect. Gabe had fixed the Suburban, her porch had been transformed, dinner out and a game of charades when they got home. The kids seemed happier. Especially Sam. And Elisabeth knew the reason.

Henry.

He was becoming more than just their farmhand; he was becoming a part of their family. The realization should have scared her more than it did. Especially since Manny had left a message while they were out to dinner saying he hoped to be coming back soon. But until *soon* arrived, Henry was still here. And that made her happy.

She heard a noise and glanced over at the barn. With Ruff tagging along at his side, Henry walked to the house. His stride exuded confidence and strength, and it was all she could do not to sigh.

Each time she saw Henry, his pull was stronger. She wanted to fight the temptation to be drawn in. That's what she should be doing. But not tonight. She wanted the magic of today to continue. She wanted to forget about her responsibilities and her fears. Just this once.

She combed her fingers through her hair. A silly, schoolgirl action, but Elisabeth didn't care. Henry had made her feel carefree and young today. Two ways she never thought she'd ever feel again.

"Having fun?" Henry asked.

"Yes." She kicked her feet out in front of her the way she had when she was a little girl. As a child, she had believed in knights in shining armor the same way her sisters did now. But she'd had to grow up fast, and there hadn't been time for girlish fantasies. After Toby had proved he was not Prince Charming, she stopped believing in happy endings altogether. Maybe that had been the wrong thing to do. Maybe those things existed. Maybe Henry… "I know you had dibs on the swing tonight, but I was hoping you wouldn't mind sharing."

A muscle twitched on his neck. He didn't move.

With an encouraging smile, she patted the space next to her. "There's plenty of room for both of us."

Henry sat, leaving space between them. Elisabeth felt a tingling in the pit of her stomach and fought the urge to inch closer to him. She couldn't deny attraction had been building between her and Henry since he arrived, but since it had nowhere to go she figured she couldn't be hurt by it.

"Where are the kids?" he asked.

"In bed," she said. "You and Gabe wore them out working on this beautiful porch."

"I'm happy you like it."

"I love it," she admitted. "Today has been such a great day."

"I hope it's the first of many."

"I don't think that's possible."

He stared at her. "Anything is possible."

"I hope so," she said wistfully.

"I know so."

Silence surrounded them. She waited for it to become uncomfortable, but that didn't happen. The quiet seemed natural, welcoming, soothing.

Henry shifted on the swing. "The only thing missing is music."

"And dancing."

He nodded.

"You know, a little music would be a nice way to end the night." She bit her lip. "Would you please sing that song you always sing in the shower?"

He drew his brows together. "I didn't know you could hear me."

"Only sometimes," she said, liking how he seemed a little embarrassed. She didn't feel so vulnerable when he was, too. "The kids don't like it when they can't hear you."

As he smiled, the corners of his eyes crinkled. "I'll make sure I sing loud enough for my audience."

"That will make them happy."

His gaze captured hers. "And you?"

A kiss would make her happier. "And me, too."

A beat passed. And another. A guarded expression crossed his face and his eyes darkened. Slowly he rose and extended his arm. "May I have this dance?"

"Dance?"

He motioned to the yard. "Underneath the stars."

So romantic. Her pulse skittered. She wanted this, but a part of her was afraid. Henry would be leaving, logic reminded. But he was here now, her heart countered. "What about music?"

"You asked me to sing." He bowed. "Your wish is my command."

Excitement rippled through her, washing away her reluctance. It was only a dance. Elisabeth took hold of Henry's hand.

He led her down the porch stairs to the front yard and placed his other hand on her waist. As he sang "What a Wonderful World," they danced. He wasn't Louis Armstrong, but Henry's voice sent shivery tingles down her spine.

Believing the words he sang wasn't hard to do. Everything seemed wonderful. The stars, the moonlight, Henry. This was the stuff dreams were made of. How could she ever thank him?

A kiss?

Too bad the kiss she had in mind wouldn't be one of gratitude. She looked away from his lips.

He finished the song, but didn't let go of her. They continued to dance, the only music the chirping of crickets. The tenderness of his gaze made her knees wobble. She was glad he held her or she might have stumbled.

But if she fell, she got the feeling Henry would catch her. That filled her with optimism. She wanted to take the chance, open herself up to the possibilities.

Maybe he was different. Maybe, despite his words, he would want them all. Maybe when Manny returned, Henry wouldn't want to leave.

He stopped dancing and let go of her.

"Thank you." Her words sounded husky. She cleared her throat. "Today— This— It's all been…wonderful."

He caressed her cheek. "You are the one who is wonderful."

She waited for him to kiss her. It's what she wanted.

What she needed. Her heart pounded so loudly she was sure he could hear it.

From the corner of her eye, she glimpsed a falling star shooting across the sky like a firework. *I wish Henry would stay.* She hadn't had time to think. The wish had popped out. Why hadn't she wished for a kiss? A wish that had a chance of coming true? Elisabeth sucked in a breath.

"It's late." Henry took a step back. The distance seemed larger than the space separating them. "You have church in the morning."

That was still hours away. But she could see in the depths of his eyes, she wasn't going to get the kiss she wanted. Something had changed. The real world had crept back in. He'd felt it and so had she.

This wasn't some enchanted evening. Henry wasn't a knight who would remain by her side forever. Dreams didn't come true. Disappointment weighed down on her.

But she had tasted a little magic today and tonight. That had been more than she'd had in the past four years. Better than nothing.

She glanced at Henry.

Or was it?

Chapter Ten

The days and nights turned into a week. One more week of backbreaking farm work. One more week of bringing smiles to the Wheelers' faces. One more week of having more fun than Henry thought possible.

Who could have thought taking on the responsibilities of this farm and this family could make him...

Not happy, Henry thought, panicked. He was not a responsible kind of guy, but he took some satisfaction in knowing he hadn't screwed up too badly.

Yet.

With Elisabeth, Henry stood on the bank of the river where water for the irrigation system was drawn. The Willamette Valley skies had darkened to an ominous gray and rain fell. The weather matched the storm raging inside him.

The line between Henry the fairy godfather and Henry the man was blurring. He wanted to blame Elisabeth, but she couldn't help being so open and honest and nurturing. Not to mention beautiful. He'd wanted to kiss her so badly the night they'd danced beneath the stars in the front yard. But he'd been trying to fulfill her wish, not his own.

Henry had to remind himself of that whenever they were alone. Like now. He tried keeping their interactions light, friendly, completely nonphysical. No touching, no swinging on the porch together, nothing to put himself near her. It hadn't been easy to do, not when he thought about her each night before going to bed and every morning when he woke up.

He also felt himself getting attached to the kids. Sam, Abby and Caitlin had become happy, delightful children who were a pleasure to be around. Laughter had become as contagious as smiles this past week as they made Halloween costumes. That was exactly what Henry had hoped to accomplish.

But there was a problem.

He was beginning to feel like a Wheeler himself.

He no longer minded living on the farm. Sleeping in was a luxury he could live without. Going out to eat wasn't as good as staying in for a home-cooked meal. Using his credit card wasn't as rewarding as spending hard-earned cash. He didn't even miss champagne all that much. Though he still hated having to clean up after himself.

It didn't take an IQ the size of Abby's to realize he was in over his head, way over and about to drown if he wasn't careful. Leaving was the best option, but Manny hadn't returned. Henry couldn't leave Elisabeth and the kids alone.

He was responsible, damn it.

And this one time he couldn't pack up and hit the road.

Down at the river, Elisabeth pointed out the irrigation equipment they needed to pull out. "I can't believe I didn't remove the irrigation pump before Manny left. But we need to do it today. See the electrical wiring up there? A heavy rain could cause the water to swell, that would ruin the electrical system and we'd need to replace it."

That would cost money they didn't have, and it was already raining hard. They'd better get to work. Henry adjusted his gloves.

The Wheelers were barely scraping by. He didn't see any way for Elisabeth's life to improve if she continued with the berry farm. Farming was a lose-lose situation with prices set for harvests, payments from canneries spread out over months and intense competition from foreign produce importers. Just the fact that he'd learned that stuff in the past couple of weeks blew him away. As did watching Elisabeth refuse to give up despite the odds.

Not even money would help make a difference. That's what got him about this. Sure it would make them more comfortable and less dependent on the land, but money couldn't change the weather or the crop yields or all the other uncertainties she faced every single day working on the farm. There was no control. No stability. Only responsibility. He hated that. And wanted no part of it. But he had to help Elisabeth. He could not let her down.

She placed a pair of hip waders on the tractor. "Ready?"

Staring at the mucky water, he nodded. "I'll go in the water." Better him than her.

She drew her brows together. "Are you sure?"

No.

"Yes," he said, but she didn't look convinced. "You're better with the tractor."

"Not by much." She grinned. "You've really caught on."

"Thanks. I had a good teacher."

Henry wished her compliment didn't mean so much to him. But lately everything Elisabeth said or did seemed important. Too important. That's because she was his friend, he told himself. But would a friend's opinion matter so much? He snatched the hip waders and shoved his right foot into them.

She handed him a screwdriver. "Use this to pry open the foot valve on the suction pipe. Make sure the valve is in the down position. Once the water drains, we can pull the pipe out. Any questions?"

About a million. He gripped the screwdriver. "None."

"Be careful."

He was more afraid of disappointing her than of the water.

With a nod, Henry waded out to the center of the lake. He held the screwdriver with his teeth and lifted the pipe. It was heavier than he thought it would be. He struggled to get a good grip. It was wet and slimy and kept slipping. Using the screwdriver, he pried the valve open. Warm stinky water burst through, a poor man's version of Old Faithful, right onto his face. It tasted worse than it smelled. He clamped his mouth closed and squeezed his eyes shut.

Make sure the valve is in the down position.

He'd forgotten. At least the water was draining. That was the goal. So what if he got blasted in the face. He'd gotten the job done. A satisfied feeling settled in the center of his chest. A feeling he'd only found working on the farm. He hoped he could take it with him when he left.

"Are you okay?" Elisabeth shouted.

He nodded and hoped she could see him.

She attached the pipe to the tractor, hopped into the seat and started the engine. As the tractor moved forward on the wet ground, it heaved and slid toward the water.

It was going to roll.

Adrenaline surged. Henry took a step towards the shore, but couldn't move farther because of the suction pipe in his hands. If he let go of it that could seal the fate of the tractor and…

"Elisabeth."

Fear clawed at him. He'd never felt so useless, so helpless in his life. If she got hurt, it would be his fault. The drizzle turned into a downpour. Rain bombarded him and blurred the images in front of him.

The engine revved then almost stalled, but she didn't give up.

"You can do it," he yelled.

The water level rose, inch by inch. The continuous revving of the tractor engine prevented it from slipping again and rolling. Kept it from killing them.

A louder roar erupted when the tractor lurched forward and pulled the pipe. Henry waded to shore with it, flashed her the thumbs-up and returned to the irrigation equipment. They weren't finished yet. But the rest of the equipment came out easier.

As Elisabeth jumped out of the tractor, Henry climbed the muddy bank toward her. "You did it," he said.

A smile erupted on her face. "We did it."

Pride shot through him.

Elisabeth made her way to him. Her clothes were drenched and clinging to her in all the right places.

Her gaze met his. Only falling rain and wet clothing separated them.

Henry took her in his arms, the way he'd been dreaming of doing for days, and kissed her. Long and hard. They were wet and muddy and sweaty. She'd never tasted so warm, so sweet.

He shouldn't be kissing her. Logically that might be true, but his mind was the only part telling him to stop. The rest of him wanted to kiss her forever.

Forever?

No, for right now.

Elisabeth kissed him back with the same enthusiasm and competence as she did everything else.

Holding her in his arms and kissing her was the best thing he'd done in a long while. Well, at least since he'd first kissed her. But this…this was better than that kiss. Everything about Elisabeth kept getting better. He wanted to know everything about her. He wanted to spend every minute with her.

He wanted to keep kissing her like this. He loved it.

Loved…

Henry tore his mouth away and stepped back. Elisabeth's flushed cheeks and swollen lips made him want to kiss her again and again. He stared into her eyes, eyes filled with desire and longing for him. She was perfect, in every sense of the word.

Reality came crashing back.

He wasn't looking for perfect. He wasn't looking for forever. He wasn't even looking for right now.

But if he were, he'd found it.

Elisabeth dragged herself out of the Suburban. Two shifts at the bistro had worn her out. She wanted to shower and go to bed, but that wasn't going to happen. Henry had picked up the kids from school and watched them for her. She appreciated his help, but had no doubt total chaos would be waiting for her inside.

Standing with her hand on the back doorknob, she tried to muster an extra ounce of energy. Her night was only beginning. She would have to clean up the kitchen, straighten up the living room, stick a load of laundry in and...

Her shoulders slumped. She didn't want to think about everything she needed to do.

She opened the door and stepped inside. No food spills on the sparkling linoleum. No dishes on the gleaming countertops. Nothing out of place. The empty sink shined. Even the dish towels looked freshly washed.

This looked like her kitchen. No, this was cleaner than her kitchen.

She saw some clutter on the table. Thank goodness or she would have thought she'd been transported to the twilight zone. A second glance showed her it wasn't a mess, but decorations. A sign read Happy Unbirthday Elisabeth and sat next to a very small, pink iced cake.

She placed her purse and jacket on one of the chairs and walked into the living room. It was clean, too. All the toys had been picked up, the videos straightened. Sam sat on the couch. The television wasn't on, but music played from the boom box.

He glanced up from the book on his lap and smiled. A smile? "Hi."

"Hi." She didn't know what else to say. "What are you reading?"

"Some stupid book."

"And you're reading it because..."

"Homework. I have to."

Except he didn't read. Not all his assignments, anyway. It was a constant complaint from his teachers that a boy as bright as Sam didn't always try.

"Oh, well, that's good," she said lamely, trying not to show her surprise.

"Actually it's not that bad." He twisted the book so she could read the cover. *The Phantom Tollbooth.* "Henry said he read it when he was my age."

Henry. Of course.

"You missed the party," Sam said, changing the subject.

"I saw," she said. "Did you have fun?"

Sam shrugged. "It was okay. Abby and Caitlin had fun. We saved you a cake."

"Thank you."

"It was Henry's idea."

Elisabeth had figured that out. Everything good that happened around here turned out to be Henry's idea. She smiled.

"He's cool," Sam said. "I hope he sticks around."

Me, too. And that concerned her. They were all too attached to Henry. Elisabeth sighed. "Where are Henry and the girls?"

"Upstairs." Sam returned to his book. Homework, she corrected.

She heard a male voice coming from her room. She peeked in. Caitlin lay on the queen-size bed while Abby and Henry sat on the edge. He was reading to them.

"And the prince kissed the princess. The two moved to his castle on the hill and lived happily ever after. The End."

Henry closed the book and placed it on the nightstand. He tucked the blankets around Caitlin and kissed her forehead. "Good night, princess."

Caitlin giggled. "Good night, fairy daddy."

Holding her breath, Elisabeth waited for Henry to say something. He didn't. He merely ruffled Caitlin's curls.

Elisabeth exhaled slowly. Henry was such a natural with children. Definite father material. No doubt about it. Surely he could feel it. No one could pretend the kind of affection he showed the kids.

Thanks to him, her brother and sisters had become happy children. The way they'd been before their parents' deaths. Henry had taught them, and her, how to laugh and live again. And she knew then what she had been fighting all along—she was falling for him.

Who was she kidding? She'd fallen, head first, and was sinking deeper.

She loved Henry.

Elisabeth never thought she could feel this way about anyone. But she did. Not after Toby. She hadn't wanted it to happen; she hadn't been looking for love. But she'd found it. With Henry.

He made everything in her life seem brighter. Better. He showed her how much she had been missing out on by keeping herself closed off. He'd unlocked her heart and her soul.

So many changes. Good changes.

She didn't know what the future held, but she didn't want to go back to the way things had been. She couldn't. And neither could the kids.

He placed his arm around Abby. "Let's practice world capitals before your bedtime."

"I know them all."

"But I don't."

Elisabeth moved out of the doorway and waited for them in the hall. Waited and hoped. Perhaps he would want her and the kids. They deserved to be happy as much as anyone else.

Henry greeted her with a smile. "You're home."

Elisabeth nodded. "To a clean house. How did that happen?"

"We helped Henry," Abby said. "He didn't think you should come home to chores."

"Thanks."

"And we had a party like they had in *Alice in Wonderland*." Her eyes twinkled with excitement. "Did you see your unbirthday cake?"

"I did," Elisabeth said. "I like the pink icing."

"That was my idea. And Caitlin's." Abby grinned. "We used my Easy-Bake Oven to cook them."

"I had Sam standing by with a fire extinguisher just in case," Henry said.

Elisabeth laughed.

"Oh, and Manny called," Abby said and headed into her bedroom.

"Manny said his mother is doing better," Henry said.

"That's great." Elisabeth was happy for Manny and his family, but also confused at the mix of emotions churning inside her. She was relieved to finally hear the news she'd been waiting for and guilty for hoping he would stay away longer. "Did he say anything else?"

"Manny will be back next week."

Next week?

That was so soon. For her and the kids and Henry…

What would he do? She started to ask, but stopped herself. The answer was written in his eyes. Henry was leaving. Just as she knew he would, but had hoped with all her heart that he wouldn't.

* * *

He was leaving.

A few days later, Henry sat at the kitchen table. Ten-thirty and the kids were at school. He and Elisabeth had accomplished enough work on the evergreen blackberries to earn a coffee break. Talk about teamwork. Quite a change from his first day on the job. But thinking about the beginning reminded him of the end.

His official adventure would end in three days, but he wouldn't leave the farm until Manny returned. Henry kept telling himself that was good enough. Elisabeth didn't need two farmhands. Not with winter approaching. But the turmoil inside of Henry surprised him. He never thought he would feel this way when the day arrived to say goodbye.

And it was almost that time.

Next week he would be home.

Home.

The word didn't hold much appeal. His estate was large, with all the creature comforts anyone could imagine. Laurel Matthews and her interior design studio had seen to that during the massive remodel. But compared to this rundown farmhouse filled with kids, clutter and animals, his elegant home and exciting life were suddenly, strangely, unappealing.

But this wasn't his life. He wasn't a farmer no matter how well he'd adjusted to the work. And the Wheelers weren't his family.

He belonged to another world, one totally separate from the one he'd been living in during his adventure. Though his real life had seemed inconsequential and meaningless after just one day on the farm.

Could Cynthia be right?

Maybe he needed to rethink his over-the-top birthday parties and adventures. Maybe he needed to rethink a lot of things. He swirled the coffee in his mug.

But first Henry needed to tell Elisabeth he would be leaving. He'd tried, on more than one occasion, but the words wouldn't come. He had stared into her blue eyes and wondered how it would feel to see them cloud with passion when he made love to her. He had imagined waking up each morning gazing into them as their years together passed by. His thoughts had rendered him speechless.

But those things were simply fantasies that would never come true. He was playing a role here. Henry the farmhand was simply a disguise, a masquerade so to speak. He'd been able to step out of his real world for a few weeks and see another side. Yes, it had been liberating, but his real life was back in Portland. His real self was someone Elisabeth would never want to spend the rest of her life with.

He couldn't deny the truth. She hadn't asked him what his plans were. She hadn't said much about Manny returning. But sadness had descended over her, and that concerned Henry. They were tiptoeing around, trying to avoid the subject, but the tension was going to crack sooner rather than later. He downed the rest of his coffee.

The telephone rang and Elisabeth answered it. "Hello." She paused. "Yes, this is her. What?" The horror in Elisabeth's voice made him look up. Her ghost-pale face had him rising from the table. She clutched the receiver until her knuckles went white. "W-which hospital?"

Hospital?

A million and one thoughts raced through Henry's mind. None of them good. He walked toward Elisabeth never taking his eyes off her. Her lower lip trembled. She reached out for him.

Not one of the kids. It couldn't be one of the kids. He laced his fingers with hers and listened.

"Did she say—?"

She. Abby or Caitlin? His stomach knotted, twisting and turning until he thought he would be physically ill.

"No, I understand," Tears welled in her eyes. "I'll be right there."

As she hung up the telephone, she took a deep breath. "Caitlin fell off the play structure at preschool. She hit her head. Or they think she did. She was unconscious. They've taken her to the hospital. I—I have to go."

"Let's go."

She grabbed her bag. "My keys?"

"I've got them." Henry grabbed her ring of keys off the counter. "I'll drive and you can navigate."

Her hands trembled. "Thank you."

She said the words, but he could see she was simply going through the motions. He couldn't imagine what was going through her head, not with what he was feeling. Driving kept him from losing it all together. All he could think of was his tiny princess in a deep sleep. Only a kiss wasn't going to wake her up. Henry hoped the doctors could.

The drive to the county hospital seemed to take forever. He tried to stay focused and get them there in one piece. This wasn't the time for making mistakes. Not with so much at stake. Still a continuous stream of questions played in his head. Why wasn't someone watching Caitlin? How did she fall? What sort of head injury? How long had she been unconscious?

Henry glanced over at Elisabeth. She sat with her hands clasped on her lap. Her face was drawn tight, her entire body stiff.

He was worried sick. She must feel…

"How are you doing?" he asked.

Stupid question, but he didn't like that she was so quiet.

"I—I don't know." She blinked. "I just wish we were with her."

He removed his right hand from the steering wheel and touched her, trying to offer a small amount of comfort and reassurance. "We'll be there soon."

"I'm glad you're driving. I don't think I could have…." Her voice cracked and so did his heart. "Caitlin's never been afraid of heights. She loves to climb. She was so excited when she first went to the preschool and saw the play structure. I should have told her to stay off the top, but I never thought she'd fall."

"Caitlin would have climbed to the top even if you told her not to. She's a kid."

"Probably, but…" She choked on a sob. "What if she never wakes up? What if I lose her, too?"

Caitlin had asked him to be her daddy and he'd said no. What if he'd said yes? Regrets assailed him. He swallowed his anger to concentrate on Elisabeth. "Let's wait until we speak with the doctor before thinking the worst."

"You're right," Elisabeth said. "I know you're right."

He hoped so.

Henry parked the Suburban outside the emergency entrance of the county hospital. Elisabeth met him around the back of the car. Tears spiked her eyelashes, and he laced his fingers through hers. She squeezed his hand. "I'm so glad you're here with me."

"Me, too." He expected her to let go of his hand, but she didn't. Hand-in-hand they walked into the hospital with the same thought on both their minds—Caitlin.

Chapter Eleven

As Elisabeth made her way to the information desk, she remembered making this same journey almost four years ago with Caitlin in her arms and Sam and Abby at her sides. By the time they'd arrived, their parents were dead.

Tears stung Elisabeth's eyes, but she blinked them away. Thank goodness for Henry. He was her strength and her rock. She loved him. Pure and simple. He would be leaving, but he was here now. She clung to that.

"May I help you?" a smiling white-haired volunteer in a pink jacket asked.

"I'm looking for Caitlin Wheeler." Elisabeth tried to keep her voice steady. "She was brought in from the Berry Kids Preschool in Berry Patch."

"Oh, yes." The smile disappeared from the woman's face, and Elisabeth's pulse sped up. "Please take a seat. It'll be just a moment."

The waiting room was empty, but she didn't want to sit. That's what she'd done the last time. "Do you mind if we stand?"

"Whichever you prefer." The woman rose.

A shiver of doom inched down Elisabeth's spine. They had done the same with her parents. "This isn't good."

"Hang in there." Henry squeezed her hand. "Caitlin will be okay."

A young, handsome male doctor dressed in green scrubs walked up to them. "I'm Doctor Terrence. Are you Caitlin's parents?"

"I'm Elisabeth Wheeler, Caitlin's sister and guardian."

"Caitlin suffered a closed head trauma," he explained in a soothing tone. "There was a blow to her skull and a bruising of the brain—a concussion. She initially lost consciousness, regained it and complained of a bad headache when she woke up, and is now unconscious again. X-rays show a skull fracture and that, with her history, suggests a possible epidural bleed."

Elisabeth wanted to shake him to upset his smooth self-possession. This was her baby sister he was talking about.

"We aren't equipped to handle such traumas at this hospital," Dr. Terrence continued. "We need to get her to Portland children's hospital as soon as possible. Transportation is being arranged and a team of specialists, including a neurosurgeon, will be waiting."

"Whatever you need to do, do it." Her voice sounded shrill. She cleared her throat. "I just want her to get better."

Henry tightened his fingers around hers. She was so thankful he was with her. She couldn't imagine going through this alone.

"We're doing everything we can," Dr. Terrence said. "It's imperative we move quickly. Do you have insurance?"

"Forget about what this costs," Henry interrupted. "What's important is getting Caitlin the best care available. Right, Elisabeth?"

All she could manage was a nod. But Henry was right. If it took selling the farm, selling everything to do it, so be it. All that mattered was Caitlin.

"You can see her while we make final preparations," Dr. Terrence said.

Elisabeth and Henry followed the doctor through a set of double doors. In the center of the emergency department, doctors and nurses milled around a busy hub containing computers and monitors and phones. Around the perimeter of the central area were glass-enclosed examining areas. The doctor opened a sliding glass door to one of the rooms.

Caitlin lay on a gurney, a bandage on the side of her head. Machines beeped and blinked. No, this couldn't be happening. Not to Caitlin. Not to her baby. Anguish seared Elisabeth, weakened her knees and she collapsed against Henry. He embraced her, sharing his strength and comfort. She needed both from him. And so much more.

"She's so pale. So little." Elisabeth reached out and touched Caitlin's ashen skin. "She feels cold. Do you think she needs another blanket?"

Henry pulled up a chair for Elisabeth to sit on. "I'll find a nurse."

She sat, but didn't know what to do. She reached for her sister's small hand.

"It's going to be okay, sweetie." An IV ran into the other arm. A lump formed in Elisabeth's throat, but if she cried it would be all over with. "We're going to a hospital in Portland."

No response. Fear shuddered through Elisabeth. It was all she could do not to fall into a heap on the gray tile floor. But she couldn't. She had to be strong for Caitlin.

"Portland is where Henry used to live," Elisabeth said.

She glanced at the nurses' station in the center of the emergency department. Henry spoke to a group of people. A woman dressed in a suit handed a phone to Henry. He looked serious. A little too serious. Elisabeth looked away. She couldn't deal with any more bad news right now.

"Henry's here." She touched Caitlin's rose-petal smooth cheek. "He's making sure the doctors take good care of you. And he's taking good care of me, too."

Elisabeth kissed Caitlin's hand. She was afraid to touch anything else.

"You're going to get better." The machines continued to beep and blink. All good signs, she assumed. "Don't worry. It's going to be okay, princess. You're going to be fine."

She had to be. Because if not, Elisabeth didn't know what she would do.

As Henry watched Elisabeth, her misery and pain pressed down on him like a steel girder. It wasn't fair. She didn't deserve this. And Caitlin… She should be smiling and giggling and jumping around. A hospital bed was no place for such a vibrant little girl.

He had more money than he knew what to do with, yet he couldn't make her better. He couldn't buy his way out of this situation. Sure, Caitlin would have the top specialists and the best care available and it wouldn't cost the Wheelers anything. He'd seen to that. If only he could do more....

Elisabeth's gaze locked with his. The weight of the world once again rested on her tired shoulders and there wasn't a damn thing he could do. It took every ounce of Henry's strength to smile, but he did.

For her sake.

Doctor Terrence returned with a nurse. "Caitlin's blood pressure is increasing. This could mean the pressure in her brain is also increasing. She needs to go now." He emphasized the last word. "A Life Flight helicopter is on its way. Everything will be ready for Caitlin when she arrives at the hospital."

Elisabeth's lower lip quivered. Henry placed his arm around her and led her outside.

Standing there, she wrapped her arms around her chest. "I'm scared."

"Me, too." Henry pulled her close. "Brett and Laurel Matthews will be waiting for you at the hospital. They are my closest friends, next to Cynthia. They'll keep you company until I arrive."

Elisabeth stepped away from him. "You aren't going with me?"

Her disappointment stabbed at him. "There isn't room on the Life Flight helicopter for us. Another helicopter will follow that one, but they only have space for one passenger."

"They do that?"

"In certain instances." He didn't want to tell the truth. That he'd made the arrangements for the second helicopter so Elisabeth wouldn't have to be away from Caitlin that long. "I'll pick up Sam and Abby from school.

They need to hear what happened from one of us, not a schoolteacher or administrator."

Elisabeth nodded. "And I need someone to watch the farm—"

"I called Gabe. He and his father are on it."

More than gratitude shone in her eyes, and he felt like he'd been run over by the Deere. The edges of her mouth curved slightly. "Thank you."

Don't thank me, he wanted to yell. This was driving him crazy. The feeling of helplessness was overwhelming and he hated it. He hated feeling so useless. He hated caring the way he did. About Caitlin and Sam and Abby. But most especially about Elisabeth.

She caressed his cheek. "I don't know what I'd do without you."

He felt the same way, but he couldn't bring himself to say the words. No matter how he felt about Elisabeth and the rest of the Wheelers, she didn't need him blurting out his feelings, diverting attention from the sister she loved. The sister she had gladly taken responsibility for, the way he had never taken responsibility for anything or anyone in his life.

More people entered Caitlin's room. The doctor barked orders. Nurses hurried. Things happened so fast. Suddenly Caitlin was being wheeled out of the room on the gurney.

"Let's go," Dr. Terrence said, his voice full of urgency.

Henry walked with them until he was told he could go no farther. He wanted to go with them. He wanted to be there for them.

"Have a safe flight." Henry didn't know what else to say. "I'll be at the hospital as soon as I can."

That's all he could promise her. Once again, it wasn't enough.

As Elisabeth, the doctors and the nurses disappeared behind a pair of elevator doors, a deep pain gnawed at him. Henry waited until he figured they must have lifted off and weren't coming back. He walked to the hospital lobby, found a pay phone and made a collect call.

"I wondered when I would be hearing from you," Cynthia said, sounding smug and satisfied. "How's your adventure going down on the farm?"

Only two words needed to be said, but he was having a difficult time saying them. He didn't understand. He'd made the right choice. The right choice for Caitlin. The right choice for Elisabeth. The right choice for him. Henry knew that in his heart, but his life would never be the same. Maybe that's why this was so hard. He inhaled deeply and exhaled slowly.

"Henry?" Cynthia asked.

It was now or never. "You win."

Elisabeth was lost. She must have made a wrong turn when she walked out of the rest room. Or several.

She felt as if she were going in circles. Of course, she'd felt the same way ever since the neurosurgeon here in Portland had spoken to her. Caitlin had an acute bleed that was putting pressure on her brain. She needed surgery. Something about a pressure probe being inserted into her skull. Relieving pressure by evacuating the hematoma. It was all very confusing and frightening.

The doctor had talked about risks—death, permanent brain damage, permanent nerve damage—and alternatives to surgery—none. That had been over an hour ago. Elisabeth shivered.

Where was Henry? She wished he would arrive.

She passed a dozen pink roses in a crystal vase and

a stuffed pony sitting on the top shelf of a cart. Caitlin would love the stuffed animal. If only she were here to see it…. Emotion clogged Elisabeth's throat.

Standing at an intersection of three hallways, she decided to go straight. The left and right hallways hadn't led her to the waiting room where she'd left Laurel and Brett Matthews, friends of Henry. Elisabeth needed to get back. She needed news about Caitlin's status. She needed Henry.

What was keeping him?

She couldn't wait to see him. Henry would make her ignore the antiseptic smell in the air. He would make her see things weren't as horrible as they seemed. He would make her feel better.

The sound of her work boots against the sanitary tile floor echoed through the hallway. She walked past a bank of elevators. Again.

Her shoulders slumped. Maybe if she waited someone could show her the way. She leaned against the wall and noticed a bronze plaque engraved with a dedication hanging opposite her.

The C. & L. Davenport Wing of Portland children's hospital was donated by Henry Davenport in memory of his parents, Charles and Lillian Davenport.

Henry…Davenport? Her Henry Davenport?

It couldn't be. Henry had nothing. And yet…hadn't his friend, Cynthia, said he'd lost everything? Maybe before his misfortune Henry had…donated a whole hospital wing?

Elisabeth bit her lip, confused. It wasn't possible.

Yet if it were him...

To go from all that to nothing. Pride in Henry overflowed. After losing all that, he hadn't given up. He'd taken the job at her farm and kept going. Her respect for him grew tenfold. As did her love. She touched Henry's name on the plaque.

The elevators opened and a nurse dressed in blue scrubs exited. Elisabeth jerked her hand away from the engraving. "Excuse me, do you know how to get to the waiting room?"

The nurse nodded. "Down this hall and make the first left and another right."

"Thanks." Elisabeth glanced back at the plaque. She had to know. She didn't want to embarrass Henry by asking Brett and Laurel, but...

"Do you know him?" Elisabeth asked impulsively, half expecting to be told Henry Davenport was a carbon copy of Mr. Jackson, a balding, rotund businessman in his sixties. "Henry Davenport."

"Yes, he's very generous, especially when it comes to children. He drops off presents for the patients here," the nurse explained. "The kids call him their fairy godfather."

Caitlin had called him "fairy daddy." Elisabeth thought about everything Henry had done for them this past month. Her heart lurched. A coincidence.

"That's thoughtful of him," Elisabeth said weakly.

The nurse nodded. "Did you know he donated money for a new neonatal intensive care unit? They break ground next month."

That didn't make any sense. Not if it was her Henry. Elisabeth's spirits brightened. "Really?"

"Surprising, I know." The nurse grinned. "You'd never think someone like him would care so much about children. I mean he's a rich playboy who dates famous models and actresses and pretty much anything with a decent pair of legs."

A rich playboy?

It couldn't be. He couldn't be. Yet…

Elisabeth struggled to breathe. "I had no idea."

"You must not read the society page, then, honey. He's always in there and never with the same date." The nurse checked her pager. "I have to go."

So did Elisabeth. She needed to ask the Matthews about Henry. They were nice. They would explain what was going on.

She hurried down the hall and followed the nurse's directions to the waiting room. Maroon and forest-green modular furniture offered plenty of seating choices. A muted television set was tuned to a financial channel. The sedate and calming wall color made the room feel cozier and less institutional.

Laurel Matthews, interior designer and mother of Henry's goddaughter Noelle, straightened the skirt of her gray dress. Her blue eyes clouded with concern. "We were getting worried."

Elisabeth was worried, too. "I got lost." In more ways than one. "Any word?"

"No." Brett Matthews, financial advisor and all-around nice guy, stood. He was as handsome as his wife was beautiful. His dark brown hair curled on the ends and his chocolate brown eyes softened every time he looked at Laurel. "Would you like a cup of coffee or a soda?"

"No, thanks." Elisabeth wiped her sweaty palms on her faded and torn blue jeans. "But I would like to talk to you about Henry."

"What do you want to know?" Brett asked.

She stopped biting the inside of her cheek. She had to be wrong, simply letting her imagination run wild. "If Henry lost all his money and is homeless, how can he afford to build a new neonatal intensive care unit for this hospital?"

The troubled glance shared by Laurel and Brett told Elisabeth she wasn't going to like the answer.

"You should probably sit down," Laurel said.

Elisabeth sat, took a deep breath and prepared herself. For what, she didn't know. But from the looks of things, it wasn't going to be good.

Laurel sat next to her. "Henry means the world to Brett and I. He's a generous, caring man who loves to have a good time."

"*Fun* is Henry's middle name," Brett added.

"But he's also a bit…eccentric. A cross between Cupid and a fairy godfather," Laurel explained. "Every year, Henry throws himself an elaborate birthday party and creates wild adventures to send two friends on so he can play matchmaker. That's how Brett and I met. Cynthia Sterling and Cade Waters, also."

Elisabeth was only more confused. "How can Henry afford to do that if he lost everything? I don't understand."

"Henry didn't lose all his money." Brett sat on the other side of her. "He hasn't lost any."

Apprehension grew. "He has…money?"

"Henry is extremely…well off," Brett said.

A rich playboy… Her mind reeled.

"Cynthia thought it was time to teach Henry a lesson for everything he's put his friends through. She decided to send Henry on his own adventure." The look in Laurel's eyes softened. With pity? "To your berry farm."

Elisabeth felt as if her breath had been cut off, as if

her chest would burst. But she held herself together. She needed to know more. She needed to know…everything.

With each of Laurel's words, Elisabeth tightened her hands until her knuckles turned white. She didn't speak. She couldn't. Not when she sat stunned, numbed by the truth.

Henry wasn't poor and homeless. He was a billionaire who got his kicks playing Cupid by sending friends on outrageous adventures together. He'd been playing games with her from the start.

Cynthia, Brett, all of the other references…they had all been a part of it. They had all…lied.

"I understand," Elisabeth said through tight lips. She had to get out of here. Now.

Another worried glance passed between Brett and his wife. Brett's eyes narrowed. "Are you okay?"

"I need to use the rest room." Elisabeth picked up her purse and stood. "Excuse me, please."

Laurel rose. "Want some company?"

"No…thanks." A faint hysteria laced the words. As Elisabeth left the waiting room and walked into the restroom, she struggled for control.

She was not going to cry. She'd wasted too many tears on Toby. She wasn't going to do the same with Henry.

He'd lied to her.

She ached with a pain so ragged, so deep she feared the hurt would never go away.

Everything had been a lie.

The laughter, the smiles, the kisses. His time on the farm had been nothing more than a rich man's adventure. A joke. A bet. Payback for the years of putting his friends at the mercy of his whims.

Toby might have broken her heart, but Henry had

shattered it beyond repair. That wasn't the worst part. This time, the kids were involved. Sam, Abby and Caitlin had fallen in love with Henry. He had brought smiles to their faces, laughter to their hearts, joy to their lives. He'd changed them; he'd changed everything. The kids would be devastated.

What was she going to tell them?

She had known all along he would leave them. But she hadn't understood why. She'd even dreamed, she'd actually hoped, they could change his mind. That *she* could change his mind.

She'd been a fool.

Of course he wouldn't stay.

The nurse's words tortured Elisabeth. *He's a rich playboy who dates famous models and actresses.*

Not poor and boring farm girls from Berry Patch.

All her energy, all her strength drained. She sagged against a tiled wall. No. She couldn't give up. She would not let Henry do that to her. His lies hurt, but she would recover. So would the kids. They had no other choice.

She opened her purse and dug through her wallet until she found Cynthia's check. Elisabeth stared at all the zeros. She needed the money, especially with Caitlin's head injury, but Elisabeth couldn't keep it. The money had been given to her under false pretenses. So had the help. She ripped the check in half.

Henry's adventure was over.

He could stop lying and start laughing. About his time spent on the struggling farm. About three orphaned kids. About her.

But Elisabeth had a sinking feeling it would be a long time before she or any of the kids would feel like laughing again.

Chapter Twelve

Rain pelted the windshield, and Henry struggled to see the road. Luckily there wasn't much traffic on I-5, but once they hit Wilsonville...

He fiddled with the knobs on the radio searching for a traffic report, but heard only static. He turned it off. The two kids in the middle seat of the Suburban were quiet. "You guys okay?"

"Is Caitlin dead?" Sam asked.

Henry felt as if his heart had been ripped out of his chest. Suddenly quiet didn't seem quite so bad. "She's at the hospital."

"My parents were at the hospital, but they were dead by the time we got there," Abby said. "Caitlin could be dead."

Nausea swept over Henry. He needed to be there with Elisabeth.

"Caitlin's dead, isn't she?" Sam asked. "You're just not telling us."

Henry gripped the steering wheel. "She was stable when I last saw her."

"But that was a few hours ago," Abby said. "Anything could have happened since then and we wouldn't know."

Sometimes Abby was too smart for her own good. He grimaced. "No worst-case scenario thinking. The doctors are doing everything they can."

Silence blanketed the car. Or as much silence as one could have in the middle of a rainstorm on a major interstate.

"Was Elisabeth crying when you left her?" Abby asked.

Henry weighed his options. He didn't want to upset the kids nor did he want to lie. "She was upset."

"She never cries," Abby announced.

Henry had seen Elisabeth cry. The night he'd found her in the living room air-harping. "Never?"

"Not since Toby left," Sam answered.

"Toby?" Henry asked.

"He was going to marry Elisabeth," Abby explained.

"He was a jerk," Sam said. "He dumped her."

Any man who would leave Elisabeth was definitely a jerk. The thought made Henry squirm.

"Sometimes adults have reasons for what they do even if it appears bad," he said carefully, hoping they all, especially Elisabeth, would understand his actions this past month. "Reasons maybe they can't explain or that don't make sense to kids."

"Oh, he had reasons," Sam said. "He didn't want us."

Henry glanced in the rearview mirror. "Didn't want…?"

"Me, Abby and Caitlin. And Elisabeth wouldn't leave us," Sam admitted. "She said we were a package deal and gave Toby his ring back. Then she cried for a week."

"I don't remember an entire week of crying," Abby said.

Sam gave her a lofty look. "You were too little then."

Henry barely heard their bickering. Guilt deafened him. Swamped him. He'd originally thought the same thing. But that had changed. He had changed.

The Wheelers were a package deal and one he wanted.

Up till now his life had been meaningless. His parties and adventures were fun, but nothing compared to the life he'd found on the farm. With Elisabeth.

He'd tried to avoid responsibility. He'd tried to hang on to control. He'd tried not to let any of the Wheelers get close.

He'd failed on all accounts.

"Are you going to leave, too?" Sam asked.

Henry had intended to.

But now…

The thought of losing Caitlin terrified him. He prayed she would be okay. But if she recovered and he left, wouldn't he lose her just the same? Lose her and Abby and Sam.

Lose Elisabeth.

What a jerk.

The Wheelers had welcomed him into their home, into their lives, into their hearts. They loved him for him. Not his name. Not his wallet. It's what he'd needed all along, but he hadn't known it until now. Henry might not have started out as a family man, but that's what he'd become and what he wanted to remain.

"I don't want to leave."

It was the truth. He could admit it to this boy when he'd barely acknowledged the truth to himself. Henry wanted to be a husband, a father and a farmer. The best farmer Berry Patch had ever known. He wanted it all—love, marriage and a happily-ever-after. Not only for himself, but for all of the Wheelers. Especially Elisabeth. Henry still had a lot to learn, but he was ready. He wanted the opportunity to try and be the man Elisabeth deserved in her life.

Would she be willing to give him the chance?

Bleeding controlled. Minimal edema. No obvious death of brain matter. The neurosurgeon had been pleased with the surgery and that's what kept Elisabeth from losing all hope.

In the neurosurgical ICU, she sat next to Caitlin's bed. She had yet to regain consciousness after the surgery.

Bandages covered Caitlin's entire head. Tubes and wires were attached to her body including a catheter into her head. All the beeps and noises from the machines with too many displays and graphs and buttons scared Elisabeth.

She felt as if she was hanging by a thread. She was brokenhearted and hurting because of Henry and Caitlin.

Forget about Henry. Concentrate on Caitlin. She was so small and fragile and pale. She was the one who needed Elisabeth.

"You're my little girl. I love you so much. You have to get better. I don't think I could take it if one more person I love went away." Elisabeth rested her head on the bed. The rhythm of the machines was almost hypnotic, but far from soothing. "Wake up, Caitlin. Please wake up."

Elisabeth sensed a presence behind her. Must be one of the nurses sitting in the central core area where they monitored and watched the patients. She felt a pair of hands touch her shoulders and knew. Henry. She inhaled sharply. Every muscle tensed. Relief mixed with frustration. And she wavered. But she knew after discovering the truth, that the only thing she could do was erect a wall between them to keep from being hurt more.

"Sam and Abby are in the waiting room," Henry said. "The report from the doctor sounds promising."

Elisabeth focused on the icy fear twisting in her stomach and the panic rioting inside her. "She's still not awake."

"Give her time."

Elisabeth was furious at her vulnerability to Henry. She hated that she needed his reassurance. She shouldn't want or need anything from him. "What if time is running out?"

The question stabbed at her heart. The prognosis was good, but she was still so frightened, so worried. And to have Henry show up… She trembled.

Henry squeezed Elisabeth's shoulders. "It won't."

Not for Caitlin, Elisabeth prayed. But for herself and Henry…

She wanted to hurt him but she wanted to make him want her at the same time. "I know who you are." Her voice sounded steadier than she felt. "When were you going to tell me the truth?"

He hesitated.

Loneliness and confusion, frustration and anger welded together. But she had her pride. He couldn't take that from her. "I deserved the truth. Then and now."

She felt the breath he drew.

"The truth," he agreed. "I didn't plan to tell you."

She didn't think it was possible to feel any more pain. She'd been wrong.

"Ever?" She held her own breath.

Again, that slight hesitation. "No."

Her heart died within her. She'd always known. But to hear him say it…

But she didn't fall into a heap. She didn't slump in her chair. Instead, her blood boiled, her cheeks grew hot with humiliation. She pinned him with her eyes. "You were just going to leave."

"Elisabeth…"

She pressed her lips together. "The truth."

"Okay. I was planning to leave. But—"

"I don't want to hear any of your excuses." She spat out the words. "Just go back to your real world and leave us alone."

"You are my real world." He touched her hand and she jerked away. "You, Sam, Abby, Caitlin, Ruff, Ritz, even that damn rooster who *cock-a-doodle-doos* all day long."

A part of her had longed to hear those very words and wanted to believe him. But she couldn't. This wasn't Henry, the down-on-his-luck farmhand talking. This was Henry the billionaire. The liar. "I don't believe you."

Pain cut across his face. It made her start to reach out to him, but then she drew back.

"It's the truth," he mumbled.

"But you're rich. And have a whole other life. Without us."

Without me.

Saying the words made them more real. Bitterness filled her voice. Anguish squeezed her heart. Henry might think he wanted them at first, but he would leave.

A rich playboy… Never with the same date.

"I know all about your 'adventure.'" She struggled

to hold on to her composure and her pride. "I ripped up Cynthia's check."

"What check?" Henry asked.

"The ten thousand dollars she gave me to hire you."

His eyes darkened. "That's a lot of money."

"Not to you." Elisabeth was acting like a bratty kid. She didn't care. She couldn't care. Not about him.

"Elisabeth—"

"No matter what your intentions, I appreciate you working on the farm." She straightened. "If you leave me your address, I'll mail your final paycheck."

"I don't need the check," he said. "I need you."

She shrugged, ignoring how the desperation in his voice clawed at her. She didn't know what to do. Conflicting emotions were turning her inside out. She couldn't take it. Not now. Probably not ever. "It's better this way. I know you have places to go, money to spend, women to woo."

He drew his brows together. "Woo?"

"Or whatever it is you do with them. You've been on a boring berry farm for a month. I'm sure you need to make up for lost time."

Tears stung her eyes. She focused on Caitlin so he wouldn't see. This was for the best. If Henry remained in her life, he would never be happy. He would leave her. Leave the kids, too. Elisabeth preferred he did it now.

"What are you saying?" he asked.

"Goodbye."

As she stared at one of the monitors, she waited. Beeping, blips, breathing. Then she heard it. The footsteps. Moving away from her. She listened until they were gone.

The strength she'd been clinging to vanished, leaving her lost and dejected and with nothing.

In spite of the lies, in spite of everything, a part of her had still hoped Henry would be different. That he wasn't like the others who went away or died and left her alone. She felt an acute sense of loss. Elisabeth clenched her hands into fists.

Footsteps sounded again. Only this time they were coming toward her. Closer and closer. Her breath caught in her throat.

"I'm not going to let you do this," Henry said. "I heard what you said to Caitlin about another person you loved going away. I'm not like the others. I won't leave you. And I won't let you push me away."

Elisabeth had to push. She had to be the one to send him away. Because if he was the one to leave her, she didn't think she would survive. And she had to survive. For Sam and Abby and—Elisabeth looked at the hospital bed—Caitlin.

"I've never had to fight for anything in my life, but I'll fight for you. And I won't lose."

"Don't do this." She choked on the words, battling the desperation threatening to overwhelm her. "Stop saying things you don't mean."

"I'm not going away." His eyes implored her. "I need you, Elisabeth. And the kids."

He was breaking through her fragile control. She trembled and tried to fight it, fight him. She gritted her teeth. "You lied."

He bowed his head. "I let you down."

"You lied to us. To me. At least take some responsibility and admit it."

He winced. "Okay. Yes. I lied. I'm sorry."

His admission didn't make her feel any better. Her anger surged. "It was all an act to you, wasn't it? A masquerade. Playing at being a farmhand. Acting as if you didn't mind having the kids around. Pretending you—" her voice broke "—you were attracted to me."

"No," he said. "Elisabeth, no."

"Then why not tell me the truth? Why not get that close to me?"

"Because I was afraid, all right?" The words burst out of him. He looked almost angry. "I was afraid if you knew Henry Davenport, the real me, you wouldn't want me around anymore."

"Yeah, right."

"It's the truth. My own parents—" His jaw clamped shut.

"Your own parents…what?" she asked softly.

"My own parents knew me better than anyone. And they pretty much decided I was worthless. A disappointment to the mighty Davenport legacy." His eyes darkened. "Maybe I didn't want you to think the same."

"How could I? Henry, you've made such a difference in my life. To the farm. To the kids."

To me.

"Sure, I did." He rolled his eyes. "I screwed up. All the time."

"You tried. All the time. I loved that you tried."

He regarded her somberly. "But could you love me?"

"I…" Fear closed her throat. How could she admit it knowing what she knew?

"That's what I thought."

She couldn't let him think she hadn't cared about him. Because she did. Or had. "How can I love you? A billionaire? I loved Henry the farmhand. But—"

"But that's who I am." His gaze sought hers. "At least, that's who I want to be."

His words opened Elisabeth's heart and made her want to believe him. But she was scared.

"I'm far from perfect," he explained. "But I don't want to lose you. I'll do whatever it takes to keep you."

"I can't be bought."

"This isn't about money," he said. "When I worked on the farm, I finally felt as if I had accomplished something. Not with my money, but with my hands. My heart. My soul. It was the second best feeling in the world."

"The second? What was the first?"

"Kissing you."

A monitor blipped. For a moment Elisabeth thought it was her heart. She glanced at the bed.

Caitlin's eyes fluttered opened. She looked at Elisabeth. The love in Caitlin's eyes nearly knocked Elisabeth over. Caitlin's gaze rested on Henry. "Daddy?"

The word was so faint, but Elisabeth had heard it. A wave of relief, the size of a tsunami, washed over her.

Henry covered Caitlin's hand with his. "I'm right here, princess. Daddy's right here. And I'm not going anywhere until you can come with me."

The corners of Caitlin's mouth curved, and she closed her eyes.

A nurse ran into the room. "The monitors showed some movement."

"Caitlin woke up." As Elisabeth backed away from the bed to give the nurse room, tears of joy streamed down her face. "She opened her eyes, spoke, smiled."

The nurse checked Caitlin. "What did she say?"

"Daddy." Henry's voice cracked.

The doctor arrived. Henry and Elisabeth stepped out into the hallway.

"I didn't think she was going to wake up." A sob racked her body. "I really thought we would lose her."

"Not a chance." Henry hugged her. "Caitlin's a fighter. She's strong like her big sister."

The worst seemed to be over, but Elisabeth still struggled to hold it together. Using what little remained of her willpower she stepped out of Henry's embrace. "Why did you answer when Caitlin called for daddy?"

"Because she was talking to me," he explained. "She asked if I would be her daddy a couple of weeks ago, but I didn't give her the right answer. Lucky for me, she gave me a second chance today. I wasn't going to blow it this time."

Elisabeth tried to understand what he was saying. "You want to be her daddy?"

"I do." The genuineness of Henry's words brought tears to Elisabeth's eyes. "I told you. I'm not leaving. I want to be Caitlin's daddy and a father figure for Abby and Sam. And for you—"

"I don't need a father figure."

"I was thinking more along the lines of husband."

Her mouth gaped.

"Okay, this is sudden. We've never been on a date or had a meal without the kids around. But I know it's the right thing to do and you'll have plenty of time to think about it. You can go back to college and graduate. Maybe attend a music conservatory. Play with an orchestra or two. I'll stay at the farm with the kids until you are ready to come back and get married."

As she stared at him, at Henry, realization dawned. This was no joke. It wasn't a game or an adventure. This was real. He was serious. He wanted to be a permanent fixture at the farm and in her life.

In all their lives.

Her heart swelled with joy.

Henry wasn't going anywhere. He was staying.

"You have this all planned out," she said.

"I tend to think I know what's best for…for the people I love," he said a bit defensively. "But it's a good plan."

"Are you sure this isn't just you wanting to play the fairy godfather? Or plan another adventure?"

"One hundred percent positive."

"You told me you didn't want kids."

"I changed my mind." Hope gleamed in his eyes and matched her own. "Have you changed yours?"

The easiest thing to say was "no," but Elisabeth didn't want to do that. She couldn't.

"I have changed my mind," she admitted. "I was so afraid of being left again, I've been relying on excuses to keep my heart safe. My parents, my ex-fiancé, the farm, the kids. It was easier that way. Until I met you."

Henry grinned. "You could have told me."

"Would you have believed me?"

"Probably not."

It was her turn to smile. "Because of you I opened myself up. Became a better person. A better sister."

"You've always been a great sister."

"Thanks." A warm glow flowed through her. "You made me want to live fully, to have fun, to accept help when I needed it, to take a chance on love. But—"

"There can't be a but," he interrupted.

"But you can't plan everything like its one of your adventures. You can't tell me what I should do," she explained. "We need to be able to figure things out and make plans together. Okay, Cupid-fairy-godfather Henry?"

He laughed. "I wouldn't want it any other way."

"Good, because I would like to graduate from college, but playing the harp in an orchestra is an old dream." A surprising peace settled around her heart. "My new dreams revolve around this guy named Henry who I fell in love with. He seems to think he's a berry farmer."

"I am a berry farmer." Mischief glinted in his eyes. "Or will be, once you say yes."

"Yes?"

"To my marriage proposal." Henry held her hand. "I love you, Elisabeth, and I want you to be my wife. Of course, I'd prefer to wait and propose properly with roses and a horse-drawn carriage and a tasteful, yet large diamond ring set in platinum or gold. Your choice."

"I love you, Henry. Not your money," she admitted. "I don't need something fancy or expensive."

"I know, but humor me. It'll make life a lot easier for both of us."

Elisabeth could barely breathe. She knew enough about Henry to know life was going to be interesting and different and never boring.

"You're hyperventilating." He squeezed her hand. "I take it that's a good sign?"

All she could do was nod. She didn't need any of those things he'd mentioned. Sure they were thoughtful and romantic, but all she needed was Henry. The man she loved.

"Henry Davenport, berry farmer, husband and father." He grinned. "Kind of catchy, don't you think?"

Epilogue

"Happy birthday, Daddy." Caitlin reached up to give Henry a hug. "I hope you like your party."

"I love my party." It was April Fools' Day—Henry's thirty-fifth birthday. The farm-themed party, being thrown by Sam, Abby and Caitlin, was nothing like the elaborate ones Henry used to throw for himself. This one was a million times better. Just like his life on the berry farm with his wife and the kids. He glanced at Elisabeth, who was passing out pieces of the cake she'd baked in the shape of a barn to guests. He kissed the top of Caitlin's head, a mass of blond ringlets that had grown back since her surgery. "Thank you, princess. And I love the picture you drew for me."

She beamed. "I love you."

With that she ran off to join Sam and Brett on the porch. Cynthia and Cade were inside with Sam, probably playing video games. Abby and Theresa sat on a blanket in the front yard and played with Noelle while Laurel talked to Gabe. Laurel already had lots of ideas for the interior of the house Henry and Elisabeth were having Gabe build. The current farmhouse was crowded enough, and once the baby arrived…

Henry smiled. Family, friends, the farm. He had so much and wanted everyone to be as happy. He stared at Gabe. Such a great guy, and single, too. There had to be a woman out there for him.

"You seem a million miles away," Elisabeth said.

"I was thinking that Gabe deserves to find the right woman, like I did. He'd be a lot happier, don't you think?"

"Maybe." Elisabeth smiled. "But your days of sending friends on adventures are over."

"I know," Henry admitted. "I wouldn't have time to do it anyway now. But I wish everyone could experience what we have together."

"You're too sweet." She brushed her lips against his. "But remember, no matchmaking."

"Cynthia won't let me forget."

"Good for her," Elisabeth teased. "And Gabe."

Henry nodded, but an idea was taking shape in his mind. He couldn't play matchmaker, but surely no one would mind if he provided Gabe with an introduction or two.…

* * * * *

SILHOUETTE *Romance* ®

In a
Fairy Tale
World...

Six reluctant couples.
Five classic love stories.
One matchmaking princess.
And time is running out!

Playing matchmaker is hard work— even for royalty!

The latest couple: A rich and sexy Latino doctor may be many women's dream, but not for Jane-of-all-trades Ruthie Fernandez. This young widow had her happy marriage and now only wants to care for her beloved mother-in-law...until the heat between her and Diego begins to burn down her heart's barriers!

RICH MAN, POOR BRIDE
by Linda Goodnight
Silhouette Romance #1742
On sale November 2004!

Only from Silhouette Books!

**The bonds holding the Stone Gods
are weakening…and all are in danger…**

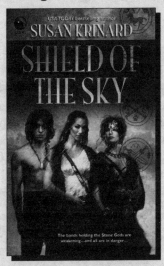

The mountain dwelling shape-shifters—partners to the
Free People—are disappearing, and word has come of
an evil new god: The Stone God.

Rhenna of the Free People, isolated by her tribe,
walks alone guarding the land's borders. When she
hears that a shape-shifter has been captured, she knows
she must rescue him.

Now, embroiled in a dangerous game as the forces of evil
and nature fight to control humanity's future, Rhenna must
travel the world, seeking to prevent its destruction.

On sale October 2004.

LUNA™

Visit your local bookseller.

More Than Words

Ordinary women…extraordinary compassion

Harlequin celebrates the lives of women who give back to their communities. Five bestselling authors come together in MORE THAN WORDS, a collection of fictional romantic stories inspired by these dedicated women.

These entertaining stories will warm your heart and lift your spirits.

All net proceeds from this book will be reinvested in Harlequin's charity work.

Available October 2004 at your local retailer.

HARLEQUIN

More Than Words

SILHOUETTE *Romance*®

COMING NEXT MONTH

#1742 RICH MAN, POOR BRIDE—Linda Goodnight
In a Fairy Tale World...
Ruthie Ellsworthy Fernandez is determined to steer clear of gorgeous military physician Diego Vargas and his wandering ways. Ruthie wants roots, a home and a family more than anything, and though Diego's promises are tempting, they're only temporary—aren't they?

#1743 DADDY IN THE MAKING—Sharon De Vita
Danger is Michael Gallagher's middle name. But when he comes to a rural Wisconsin inn to unwind and lay low, beautiful innkeeper Angela DiRosa and her adorable daughter charm their way into his life. And soon Michael is finding that risking his heart is the most dangerous adventure of all.

#1744 THE BOWEN BRIDE—Nicole Burnham
Can a wedding dress made from magical fabric guarantee a lasting marriage? That's what Katie Schmidt wonders about her grandmother's special thread. And when handsome single father Jared Porter walks into Katie's bridal shop, she wonders if the magic is strong enough to weave this wonderful man into her life for good.

#1745 A WHIRLWIND...MAKEOVER—Nancy Lavo
Maddie Sinclair is a walking disaster! But when she needs a date to her high school reunion, her friend Dan Willis uses his photographer's eye to transform her from mousy to magnificent. With her new looks, Maddie's turning heads...especially Dan's.

SRCNM1004